The

ophile Gautier

The Romance of a Mummy

The

ophile Gautier

The Romance of a Mummy

ISBN/EAN: 9783337348731

Printed in Europe, USA, Canada, Australia, Japan

Cover: Foto ©Andreas Hilbeck / pixelio.de

More available books at **www.hansebooks.com**

THE

ROMANCE OF A MUMMY.

TRANSLATED FROM THE FRENCH OF THÉOPHILE GAUTIER

BY

AUGUSTA McC. WRIGHT.

PHILADELPHIA:

J. B. LIPPINCOTT & CO.

1882.

THE ROMANCE OF A MUMMY.

PROLOGUE.

"I HAVE a presentiment that we shall find a tomb intact in the valley of Bibán-el-Molook," said a young Englishman of haughty mien to an individual of much more humble appearance, who was engaged in mopping, with a huge blue-checked handkerchief, his bald head, from which the perspiration was oozing as though it were made of porous clay and filled with water like a Theban gargoulette.

"Osiris hear you!" said the German doctor to the young lord. "This invocation is certainly permissible opposite the ancient Diospolis Magna; but we have failed so often,—the treasure-seekers have always been ahead of us."

"If we can but find a tomb untouched by the Shepherd Kings, the Medes of Cambyses, Greeks, Romans, or Arabs, that will yield up to us its treasures and mysteries inviolate!" continued the perspiring savant, with an enthusiasm that made his eyes sparkle behind his blue spectacles.

"And on the subject of which you will publish a

3

most learned dissertation, that will give you a place in science beside Champollion, Rosellini, Wilkinson, Lepsius, and Belzoni," said the young lord.

"It shall be dedicated to you, my lord, it shall be dedicated to you; as, but for the royal munificence with which you have treated me, I should not have been able to corroborate my theories by a sight of the monuments, and I should have died in my village home in Germany without having feasted my eyes upon the wonders of this ancient land," replied the savant with feeling.

This conversation took place not far from the Nile, at the entrance of the valley of Bibán-el-Molook, between Lord Evandale, astride of an Arabian horse, and Dr. Rumphius, less superbly mounted on a donkey whose lean flanks a fellah was belaboring. The dahabeëh that had brought the two voyagers, and that during their stay was to serve them as a lodging, was anchored on the other side of the Nile, before the village of Luxor, the oars shipped, and the great triangular sails rolled up and tied to the yards.

After having devoted some days to visiting and studying the stupendous ruins of Thebes,—gigantic remains of a grand period,—they had crossed the river on a *sandal* (a species of row-boat), and were on their way towards the barren range of peaks that enclose in their midst, down in mysterious catacombs, the former inhabitants of the palaces on the opposite shore. Some of the crew accompanied Lord Evandale and Dr. Rumphius at a distance, while the rest, stretched on the deck in the shadow of the cabin, calmly smoked their pipes and guarded the boat.

Lord Evandale was one of those young Englishmen, irreproachable at every point, that British high life presents to civilization; bearing about him a disdainful repose of manner, the result of an immense hereditary fortune, a historic name, inscribed in the book of the *Peerage and Baronetage*, that second English Bible, and a beauty against which nothing could be said, unless that it was too perfect for a man. In fact, his purely-cut but cold features seemed a copy in wax of those of Meleager or Antinoüs. The roseate hues of lip and cheek looked as if they might have been produced by carmine and rouge, and his light-brown hair curled naturally with all the perfection of arrangement that a skilled hairdresser or clever *valet de chambre* could have effected. But the firm glance of the steel-blue eyes and a slight curl of the nether lip corrected anything that might have been too effeminate in his appearance.

Member of the Yacht Club, the young lord indulged himself occasionally in an excursion upon his own tidy little craft " Puck," built of teak wood, fitted up like a boudoir, and manned by a small crew of experienced sailors. The year previous he had visited Iceland; this year it was Egypt, and his yacht awaited him in the harbor at Alexandria. He had with him a scientist, a physician, a naturalist, a special artist, and a photographer, so that his trip might not be an unprofitable one. He was highly cultivated, and his successes in the world had not made him forget his triumphs at Cambridge University. He was attired with the perfection and scrupulous neatness characteristic of the English, who travel over the sands of the desert in the same dress that would serve them for a promenade at Ramsgate or West End. Coat, vest, and pantaloons of white linen, for the purpose of reflecting the solar rays, composed his costume, that was finished by a narrow cravat,—blue dotted with white,—and a very fine Panama hat with a gauze veil.

Rumphius, the Egyptologist, retained, even in that burning climate, the traditional black coat of the savant, with limp skirts and dilapidated collar, here and there a button frayed and some with nothing but the silk covering left. His pantaloons were shiny in spots, and showed the warp of the cloth; near the right knee an attentive observer might have remarked, on the grayish surface of the stuff, regular lines of a darker shade, showing that the savant had a habit of wiping his pen on that part of his clothing. His muslin cravat, twisted in a string, hung loosely around his throat, remarkable for the prominence of that cartilage vulgarly known as Adam's apple. Though dressed with a scientific negligence, Rumphius for all that was not handsome: a few reddish locks, sprinkled with gray, clustered around his widely-separated ears and protested against the unnecessary height of his coat-collar; his pate, en-

tirely bald, shone like ivory, and overhung a nose
of prodigious length, spongy and bulbous at the end,
a conformation that, joined to the blue disks of his
spectacles, gave him a vague resemblance to an ibis,
increased by his stooping shoulders,—an appearance
quite in keeping with, and almost providential for,
a decipherer of hieroglyphics. It seemed as if an
ibiocephalous deity, like those depicted in the frescoes of the sepulchres, had found its way by means
of metempsychosis into the body of a savant.

Lord Evandale and the doctor proceeded on their
way towards the rocky peaks surrounding the valley
of Bibán-el-Molook, the royal necropolis of ancient
Thebes, continuing the conversation of which we have
given a part, when, like a troglodyte from the black
jaws of an empty tomb, an ordinary dwelling of the
fellahs, a new personage, clad in rather a theatrical
fashion, entered brusquely upon the scene. He
stopped before the travellers, and saluted them with
that gracious salutation of the Orientals, at the same
time humble, flattering, and dignified. He was a
Greek, who took contracts for excavations, a mer-
chant and manufacturer of antiquities, selling the new
when he had none of the old on hand. Nothing
about him, however, betokened the eager and vulgar
impostor. He wore the *tarboosh* of red felt, with a
long blue silk tassel falling over the back of it, and
beneath the narrow edge of the inside skull-cap of
thick white linen his shaven temples were visible,
tinged like a cheek from which the beard has just

been shorn. His olive skin, black eyebrows, aquiline nose, hawk-like eyes, heavy moustaches, and chin nearly cleft in two by a dimple that looked as if it might have been the work of a sabre, would have given him the veritable physiognomy of a brigand, if the fierceness of the features had not been tempered by the bland manner and servile smile of the speculator frequently brought into contact with the public. His costume was very neat: it consisted of a cinnamon-colored jacket, braided with silk of the same shade, leggings of the same material, a white vest, with buttons that looked like chamomile flowers, a wide red sash, and very full pleated breeches. The Greek had been watching for some time the dahabeëh anchored before Luxor; and from the number of the crew, the magnificence of the establishment, and, above all, the English colors floating from the stern, he had scented with his mercantile instinct some rich traveller, whose scientific curiosity might be turned to account, and who would not be satisfied with statuettes of blue or green enamelled ware, engraved scarabæi, hieroglyphic cartouches printed on paper, and other small specimens of Egyptian art. He followed the going and coming of the voyagers among the ruins, and, knowing that they would not fail, after their curiosity was satisfied, to cross the river and visit the royal catacombs, awaited them on his own ground, certain that they would not leave him empty-handed. He considered this domain of the dead as his own property, and dealt summarily with all the miserable little jackals that took it into their heads to scratch among the tombs.

With the characteristic shrewdness of the Greeks, he immediately calculated Lord Evandale's probable revenues from his appearance, and made up his mind to be perfectly frank with him, believing that he would gain more by the truth than by lies.

He also gave up all idea of leading the Englishman through catacombs that had been visited already scores of times, and decided that no excavations should be made in places that he knew were quite empty, having removed all the contents, and disposed of them at a good price, long ago.

Argyropoulos (for that was the name of the Greek), in exploring some parts of the valley, not so often tested as others, because excavations in that direction had not been attended with any success, had come to the conclusion that, at a certain point behind some rocks, whose arrangement seemed due to chance, there existed without doubt the entrance to a *syrinx*,* hidden with unusual care, which his great experience in this kind of search made him recognize by a thousand indications, imperceptible to eyes less practised than his, that were clear and piercing as those of the sacred hawk perched upon the entablatures of the temples.

For two years since making this discovery he took pains never to walk or to glance in that direction, fearing to arouse the suspicions of the violators of the tombs.

---

* *Syrinx*, a subterranean burial-place.

"Would your lordship like to make any excavations here?" asked the Greek Argyropoulos, in a species of cosmopolitan patois, the peculiar consonances and syntax of which we shall not attempt to reproduce, but which may be easily recalled by those who have visited the ports of the Levant and have had occasion to employ the polyglot dragoman who has nothing but a jumble of languages at his command. Happily, the idioms used by Argyropoulos were familiar to Lord Evandale and his learned companion. "I can place at your disposal a hundred intrepid fellahs, who, incited by a *corbag** and backsheesh, would dig down to the bowels of the earth with their finger-nails. We might tempt them to bring to light some buried sphinx, to clear away the obstructions before a temple, to open a tomb——"

Seeing that his lordship was not dazzled by these enticing proposals, and that an ironical smile passed over the lips of the savant, Argyropoulos understood that he was not dealing with ready dupes, and decided that he would sell to the Englishman the discovery that he counted upon to round off his own little fortune and furnish a marriage-portion for his daughter.

"I perceive that you are learned men and not mere travellers, and that commonplace curiosities would have no charm for you," he continued, in an English freer from Greek, Arab, and Italian idioms, "so I will show you a tomb that up to this time has escaped

---

* *Corbag,* a whip made of hippopotamus-hide.— *Wilkinson.*

the investigations of treasure-seekers, and that is un-known to any one but myself; it is a prize that I have guarded carefully for one who should prove worthy of it."

"And for which you will make us pay a round sum," said his lordship, smiling.

"I will not hide from your lordship that I expect a good price for my discovery; every one in this world gets his living as he can. I unearth Pharaohs and sell them to strangers. Pharaohs are getting scarce the way things are going now, and there are not enough for all. The article is in demand, and it is no longer manufactured."

"It is true," said the scientist, "it is some centuries since the kolchytes,* taricheutes, and parischites have shut up shop, and that the Memnonia, silent quarter of the dead, has been deserted by the living."

The Greek, hearing these remarks, looked askance at the German, but, judging from his dilapidated garments that he would not have much to say in the matter, continued directing his remarks solely to his lordship.

"For a tomb dating back to remotest times, my

---

* The kolchytes, counting a certain number of priests among them, managed the business of the embalming-houses : received the bodies, took orders for embalming, paid tribute to the king, etc. They were highly respected. The tari-cheutes, the embalmers, were allowed to mingle with other citizens, though the odium of their trade clung to them. But the parischites, whose duty it was to open the bodies, were considered unclean and treated as outcasts.—TRANSLATOR.

lord, and that no human hand has disturbed since the priests rolled the rocks before the entrance three thousand years ago, is it too much to ask a thousand guineas? After all, the price is a mere nothing, as it may contain gold in the lump, necklaces of pearls and diamonds, ear-rings of carbuncle, sapphire seals, ancient idols of precious metals, the currency of the time,—that by itself would bring a good price."

"Artful scoundrel," cried Rumphius, "you are trying to increase the value of your goods; but you know better than any one else that such things are not to be found in Egyptian sepulchres."

Argyropoulos, seeing that he had to deal with people who understood their ground, ceased trying to throw dust in their eyes, and, turning to Evandale, said,—

"Well, my lord, does the bargain suit you?"

"Yes, we will call it a thousand guineas," replied the young nobleman, "if the tomb has never been touched, as you represent, and nothing, not even a stone, has been disturbed by the levers of the excavators."

"And upon condition," added the prudent Rumphius, "that we can carry away everything the tomb contains."

"I accept," replied Argyropoulous, with an air of perfect assurance: "your lordship may risk the bank-notes and gold without fear."

"My dear Rumphius," said Lord Evandale to his acolyte, "the prayer that you made a moment ago seems to have been heard: this rascal evidently knows what he is about."

"Heaven grant it!" rejoined the savant, hitching the collar of his coat up the back of his neck and letting it down again in a dubious and pyrrhonic manner ; "but the Greeks are such audacious liars! *Cretæ mendaces,* says the proverb."

"This is a Greek of the mainland, no doubt," said Lord Evandale; "and I believe that for once, at least, he is telling the truth."

The director of excavations went on a little in advance of the nobleman and the savant, with the air of a well-bred person who knows the rules of etiquette, and his step was firm and brisk, as though he were quite confident of success. They soon reached a narrow defile leading into the valley of Bibán-el-Molook. It looked as if it had been cut by the hand of man through the thick wall of the mountain instead of being a natural cleft, as if the spirit of solitude had sought to render inaccessible this kingdom of the dead. On the perpendicular walls of the riven rock the eye could discern imperfect remains of sculptures, injured by the ravages of time, that might have been taken for inequalities of the stone, aping the crippled personages in a half-effaced bas-relief. Beyond the gorge the valley widened a little, presenting a spectacle of the most mournful desolation. On either side rose in steep crags enormous masses of calcareous rock, corrugated, splintered, crumbling, exhausted, and dropping to pieces in an advanced state of decomposition under the implacable sun. These rocks resembled the bones of the dead, calcined on a funeral pyre, and an eternity of weariness was expressed in the yawning mouths, imploring the refreshing drop that never fell. Their walls rose almost in a vertical line to a great height, marking out their indented tops of a grayish-white against a sky of deepest indigo, like the turrets of some gigantic ruined fortress. A part of the funereal valley lay at a white heat under the rays of the sun ; the rest was bathed in that crude bluish tint of torrid lands, which seems unreal at the North when artists reproduce it, and which is as clearly defined as the shadows on an architectural plan. The valley lengthened out, now making an angle in one direction, now entangling itself in a gorge in another, as the spurs and projections of the bifurcated chain advanced or receded. According to a peculiarity of climates where the atmosphere, entirely free from moisture, possesses a perfect transparence, aerial perspective did not exist in this theatre of desolation ; every little detail was sketched in, as far as the eye could reach, with a painful accuracy, and their distance made evident only by a decrease in size, as if a cruel nature did not care to hide any of the poverty or misery of this barren spot, more dead itself than those whom it covered.

Over the wall, on the sunny side, fell a fiery stream of blinding light such as emanates from metals in a state of fusion. Every rocky surface, transformed into a burning mirror sent it glancing back with even greater intensity. These reacting rays, joined to the scorching beams that fell from the heavens and were reflected again from the earth, produced a heat equal to that of a furnace, and the poor German doctor constantly sponged his face with his blue-checked handkerchief, that looked as if it had been dipped in water. You could not have found a handful of soil in the whole valley, so there was no blade of grass, no bramble, no creeping vine of any kind, nor growth of lichen, to break the uniform whiteness of the torrefied ground. The crevices and dents in the rocks did not contain enough moisture to feed even the slender thread-like roots of the poorest wall-plant. It was like a vast bed of cinders left from a chain of mountains burnt out in some great planetary fire in the day of cosmic catastrophes: to make the comparison more complete, long black streaks, like scars left by cauterizing, ran down the chalky sides of the peaks. Absolute silence reigned over this scene of devastation; not a breath of life disturbed it; there was no flutter of wings, no hum of insects, no rustling of lizards or other reptiles; even the tiny cymbal of the grasshopper, that friend of arid wastes, could not be heard. A sparkling, micaceous dust, like powdered sandstone, covered the ground, and here and there formed mounds over the stones dug from the depths of the chain with the relentless pickaxes of past generations and the tools of troglodyte workmen, preparing under ground the eternal dwelling-places of the dead.   The fragments torn from the interior of the mountain had made other hills, friable heaps of stones, that might have been taken for a natural ridge.   In the sides of the rock were black holes, surrounded by scattered blocks of stone,—square openings flanked by pillars covered with hiero-glyphics, and having on their lintels mysterious car-touches that contained the sacred scarabæus in a great yellow disk, the sun as a ram's head, and the goddesses Isis and Nephthys, standing or kneeling.

These were the royal sepulchres of Thebes.   How-ever, Argyropoulos did not stop here, but led the travellers up an ascent that seemed at first like a scaling off of the rocky surface, obstructed now and then by *débris*, to a sort of platform jutting out from the perpendicular wall, where the blocks of stone looked as if they might have fallen there by chance, but on closer examination it was plain that they had been grouped together with some care.   When Lord Evandale, accustomed to athletic feats, and the less agile scientist had managed to climb up beside him, Argyropoulos pointed with his staff to a huge rock, and said, with an air of triumphant satisfaction, " It is there !"

Argyropoulos clapped his hands in the Oriental style, and instantly, from the clefts of the rocks and the recesses of the valley, came running lean and ragged fellahs, flourishing in their bronzed fists crow-bars, pickaxes, ladders, hammers, and every necessary implement; they swarmed up the steep ascent like a legion of black ants. Those who could not find standing-room on the narrow ledge, already occupied by the director of excavations, Lord Evandale, and Dr. Rumphius, hung on by their nails and thrust their toes into the crevices of the rock. The Greek made a sign to three of the most robust among them, who placed their levers under the largest stone. The muscles stood out upon their thin arms like cords, and they leaned with all their weight upon the iron bars. Finally the huge mass stirred, tottered for a few seconds like a drunken man, and, impelled by the united efforts of Argyropoulos, Lord Evandale, Rumphius, and some of the Arabs who had managed to find a footing upon the ledge, went rolling down the slope. Two smaller blocks were dislodged, one after the other, and then it was evident that the Greek had been right in his surmises. The entrance to a tomb that had undoubtedly escaped the investigations of treasure-seekers was exposed to view in all its integrity. It was a square kind of doorway hewn in the living rock; on either side stood twin pillars, having at their capitals cows' heads with the horns bent upward in the Isiac crescent. Above the doorway, resting on the imposts with their long hieroglyphic panels, was a large emblematic frame, displaying, in the midst of a great yellow disk, the scarabæus, type of immortality, and the deity with a ram's head, symbol of the setting sun. Outside of the disk were Isis and Nephthys, personifications of

b 2*

the beginning and the end, kneeling, with one leg
bent under them, the other raised to the height of
the elbow, according to the Egyptian posture, the
arms outstretched, expressing mystic wonder, and
wearing about the loins narrow aprons secured by
belts with falling ends.   Behind a wall made of
crude bricks and pebbles, that yielded promptly to
the pickaxes of the excavators, they discovered a
slab that closed the passage-way to the subterranean
monument.   On the clay seal upon its surface the
German doctor, familiar with hieroglyphics, read
without difficulty the device of the kolchyte guardian of the tombs, who had closed this sepulchre,
and who alone could have pointed out its mysterious
position upon the chart of the catacombs preserved
in the priests' college.

" I begin to believe," said the delighted savant to
the young lord, " that we have bagged the game at
last, and I will revoke my unfavorable opinion with
regard to this brave Greek."

" Perhaps we are rejoicing too soon," responded
Lord Evandale, " and are about to experience the
same disappointment that Belzoni encountered when
he believed that he was the first to enter the tomb
of Menephtha Seti, but after having passed through
a maze of corridors, pits, and chambers, found only
an empty sarcophagus with a broken lid, for the
treasure-seekers had attained the royal tomb by
mining through the rock in an opposite direction."

" Oh, no !" cried the savant, "the chain is too

dense at this point, and the tomb too far removed for those accursed moles to have found their way here."

During this conversation the workmen, directed by Argyropoulos, attacked the slab before the entrance to the syrinx. In clearing away a place before the slab, so as to get their levers underneath it,—for the nobleman had commanded that nothing should be broken,—they exposed to view a number of little figurines, two or three inches in length, made of blue or green enamelled ware, showing excellent workmanship,—dainty little statuettes, placed there as funeral offerings by friends and relatives, as we lay garlands of flowers on our tombs, only the flowers soon fade, and, after three thousand years, these witnesses to the mourning of the ancients are found uninjured, for Egypt creates nothing but what is imperishable. When the slab was removed, giving access to the light of day for the first time in thirty-five centuries, a fiery breath of air escaped from the dark opening as though it led into a furnace. The heated lungs of the mountain seemed giving vent to a sigh of relief through these lips so long closed. The sunlight, entering part-way into the hall of the tomb, disclosed to view in all their brilliance of coloring the hieroglyphics in intaglio, ranged along the walls in perpendicular lines upon a blue plinth. A figure in red, with the head of a sparrow-hawk crowned with the *pshent*,* held a disk containing the

---

*Pshent, the crowns of the Thebaid and Lower Egypt united in one. Wilkinson's " Ancient Egyptians," Pl. 399, vol. iii.

winged globe, and seemed to guard the sill of the
tomb as if it were the gate-keeper of eternity. Some
of the fellahs lighted torches and went in ahead of
the travellers and Argyropoulos. The resinous
flames burned faintly in the dense and suffocating
atmosphere—concentrated for so many thousands of
years in the incandescent limestone of the mountain—
within the corridors, labyrinths, and chambers of the
sepulchre. Rumphius panted, and the perspiration
poured from him in streams. Even the impassible
Evandale flushed, and felt his temples grow moist.
As for the Greek, the fiery winds of the desert had
dried him up long ago, and he perspired no more
than a mummy.

The passage-way, following a very pure and even
vein of chalk, led towards the centre of the mountain. At the other end a second door of stone,
sealed like the first with a clay seal, proved that the
sepulchre had not been violated, and showed the
existence of a new corridor plunging still farther
down into the bowels of the mountain. The heat
became so intense that the young nobleman took off
his white coat and the doctor his black one, their
vests and shirts soon following. Argyropoulos, seeing that they breathed with difficulty, said a few
words in an undertone to a fellah, who ran to the
entrance of the tomb and brought two large sponges
that had been dipped in cold water, and the travellers, according to the advice of the Greek, held them
to their mouths, inhaling a fresher air through the

wet pores, as they do at the Russian baths when the vapor is too dense.

They attacked the door, which soon yielded.

A steep stairway, cut in the living rock, appeared at their feet. On either side of the corridor, upon a green ground finished with a blue line, were ranged processions of emblematic figurines, as fresh and vivid in coloring as if the brush had been applied the night before. They were visible a moment in the light of the torches, and then faded away like the phantoms in a dream.

Beneath these *bandelettes* of fresco-painting rows of hieroglyphics, placed one above the other like Chinese characters, and separated by lines cut in the stone, offered the sacred mystery of their enigma to science.

Along the wall where there were no hieratic signs, a crouching jackal, with outstretched paws and ears erect, and a kneeling figure in a mitre, with one hand resting on a circle, seemed acting as sentinels beside a door whose lintel was ornamented with a pair of united cartouches, supported by two female figures wearing narrow aprons and extending a feathered arm like a wing.

"The deuce!" exclaimed the doctor, stopping to take breath at the foot of the staircase, and seeing that the excavations did not end there; "are we going down to the centre of the earth? The heat increases to such a degree that we cannot be far from the infernal regions."

"No doubt," replied Lord Evandale, "they followed the vein of chalk that sinks down here in accordance with the laws of geological undulations."

Beyond the steps was another quite steep passageway. On its walls, also covered with paintings, could be faintly discerned a series of allegoric scenes, explained no doubt by the hieroglyphics inscribed beneath in the manner of a legend. This frieze ran the entire length of the passage, and lower down might be seen figurines in adoration before the sacred scarabæus and the symbolic azure-tinted serpent. In coming out of the corridor, the fellah who carried one of the torches started back suddenly. The way came to an end all at once, and a square black pit yawned at their feet.

"It is a pit, master," said the fellah, addressing Argyropoulos. "What is to be done?"

The Greek took a torch, waved it to make the flame burn brighter, and then threw it into the black jaws of the pit, leaning carefully over the edge of the opening. The torch went down, turning over and over and sputtering; soon a dull stroke was heard, followed by a shower of sparks and a puff of smoke; then the flame rose clear and bright, and the orifice shone in the darkness like the fiery eye of a cyclops.

"We are no longer ingenious," said the young lord: "these labyrinths cut up by dungeons ought to have cooled the zeal of treasure-seekers and savants."

"They did nothing of the kind, however; as some were in search of gold, and others of the truth, two of the most precious things in the world," remarked the doctor.

"Bring the knotted rope," cried Argyropoulos to the Arabs: "we will examine the sides of the pit and see if they give out a hollow sound anywhere, for the excavations must go far beyond this."

Eight or ten men grasped one end of the rope to counterbalance the other, which was thrown down into the pit. With the agility of a monkey or a professional gymnast, Argyropoulos seized the swinging rope and let himself down about fifteen feet, clinging to the knots with his hands and striking the walls with his heels. The rock, thus tested in every part, gave forth a dull, dead sound; then Argyropoulos slid down to the bottom of the pit and struck the floor with the knob of his *kandjar*, but the compact rock did not respond. Evandale and Rumphius, full of anxious curiosity, leaned over the opening, at the risk of plunging in head first, and watched every movement of the Greek with intense interest.

"Hold tight up there," called the Greek at last, wearied with his fruitless search, and he grasped the rope with both hands to clamber up again.

The shadow of Argyropoulos, thrown up against the ceiling by the light of the torch still burning at the bottom of the pit, resembled the silhouette of some misshapen bird. The bronzed face of the

Greek expressed keen disappointment, and he bit his lip under his moustache.

"Not the least sign of an underground passage," he exclaimed; "and yet the excavation cannot end here."

"Unless, indeed," added Rumphius, "the Egyptian who commanded this tomb died in some distant *nome* on a journey or in battle, and they stopped excavating, as it has sometimes happened."

"Let us hope that by not giving up our search we shall discover some well-concealed outlet," said Lord Evandale; "if not, we will try to force an intersecting passage through the mountain."

"Those confounded Egyptians were so artful about hiding their burial-crypts! They did their utmost to baffle us poor mortals, and one can imagine them laughing in their sleeves at the discomfiture of excavators," muttered Argyropoulos.

Walking along the edge of the abyss, the Greek examined, with his glance as penetrating as that of a night-bird, the walls of the little chamber above the pit. He saw nothing, however, but the familiar personages of *psychostasia*,—Osiris, as judge, seated upon his throne, holding the crook in one hand and the scourge in the other, and the goddesses of Justice and Truth leading the spirit of the departed before the tribunal of Amenti. Suddenly he turned around, as if struck with a new idea. His great experience as a director of excavations made him recollect a similar case, and, moreover, every faculty was quickened by his desire to win the thousand guineas from the nobleman. Seizing a pick from one of the workmen, he began to retrace his steps, striking blows right and left upon the surfaces of the rock, at the risk of destroying some of the hieroglyphics and spoiling the beak or wing of some sparrow-hawk or sacred scarabæus.

The wall, hammered in this manner, at last gave out a hollow sound. A triumphant exclamation burst from the lips of the Greek, and his eyes sparkled.

The nobleman and the savant clapped their hands.

"Drive in your picks here," said Argyropoulos, recovering his *sang-froid,* to the men.

In a short time they had made an opening large enough to admit the body of a man.

A gallery, cut in the rock on the other side, surrounded the pit, that had been placed there as a blind to violators, and led to a square room, whose blue ceiling was supported by four massive pillars, illuminated with those red figures in white kilts that present their profiles so often in the Egyptian frescoes.

This room opened into another with a somewhat higher ceiling, resting only on two pillars. Various subjects, the consecrated boat, the bull Apis bearing the mummy to the regions of the Occident, the judgment of the soul, the weighing of the actions of the dead in the supreme balance, and the offerings made to funeral divinities, adorned the walls and pillars.

All of these sculptures were admirably carved in low-relief, but the brush had not followed in the path of the chisel. From the care and delicacy of the work one could judge of the importance of the person who had sought to hide his tomb from the knowledge of man. After some minutes spent in examining these carvings, executed in all the purity of style of the best epoch of Egyptian art, they perceived that the apartment had no outlet, and that they had landed in a sort of *cæcum*. The air became rarefied; the torches burned dimly in an atmosphere of which they only increased the heat, and the smoke went up from them in clouds; the Greek commended himself to all the devils, as if the gift had not been made and accepted long since: but this did not mend matters. They tested the walls as before, but without any result; the dense and compact rock only gave forth a dead sound: no sign of any door, corridor, or opening of any kind!

The young nobleman was evidently discouraged, and the savant let his attenuated arms drop at his sides in a dejected manner. Argyropoulos, who began to be alarmed about his twenty-five thousand francs, manifested the most extravagant despair. However, they were obliged to retrace their steps, for the heat became positively intolerable. The party returned again into the first room, and there the Greek, who could not bear to see his golden visions fade away in smoke, examined minutely the base of the columns, to assure himself that they did not cover some artfully-concealed passage-way, or trap, that might be laid bare by removing them; for, in his despair, he confounded the solid Egyptian architecture with those fairy structures of Arabian legends. The pillars in the midst of the excavated room were hewn from the mountain, and formed a part of it, so that it would have required blasting to remove them. All hope was lost!

"And yet," suggested Rumphius, "they did not amuse themselves constructing this labyrinth for nothing. There must be somewhere a passage-way similar to that about the pit. No doubt the deceased was afraid of being disturbed by importunate individuals, and ordered his resting-place to be walled up; but perseverance can force an entrance anywhere. There may be a slab ingeniously laid in the floor, covering a direct or circuitous way to the vault, whose points of juncture we cannot see on account of the dust."

"You are right, my dear doctor," said Evandale; "those confounded Egyptians joined their stones with as much care as though they moved on hinges like our English trap-doors: so let us continue our search."

The savant's idea seemed to find favor with the Greek, who began making a tour of the room, striking the floor with his heels at every step, and making the fellahs do the same.

At last, not far from the third pillar, a dull echo caught the practised ear of the Greek, who knelt down hastily to examine the spot, sweeping aside, with a ragged burnous thrown to him by one of the Arabs, the impalpable dust strewn there in the silence and shadows of thirty-five centuries.

A fine black seam, as regular as though it were a line drawn with the aid of a ruler on an architectural plan, appeared in the floor, marking out in its course an oblong slab.

"Did I not tell you," cried the enthusiastic savant, "that the excavation could not end here?"

"Really," said Lord Evandale, with his odd British phlegm, "I have some compunctions of conscience about disturbing the last sleep of this poor unknown mortal, who felt so sure that he would rest in peace until the end of the world. Our visit will be a most unwelcome one to the host of this mansion."

"All the more so as the third person is wanting to make the presentation according to rule," replied the doctor. "However, do not let it annoy your lordship. I have lived long enough among the Pharaohs to know how to introduce you into the presence of the illustrious person inhabiting this subterranean palace."

Pincers were thrust into the narrow crack, and after some tugging the block yielded and was lifted up. A steep flight of stairs descending into the darkness lay invitingly at the feet of the impatient travellers, who rushed down it pell-mell. Succeeding the steps was a gallery, sloping downwards,

painted on both sides with figures and hieroglyphics;
at the end of this gallery a few more steps led to a
short corridor, or vestibule, before a room in the
same style as the first, but larger, and supported by
six pillars cut in the living rock. The ornamentation was richer, and the usual subjects of funereal
frescoes were multiplied on a yellow ground. Right
and left in the rock were little openings or niches
filled with figurine offerings in enamelled ware,
bronze, and sycamore wood. " We are in the ante-
chamber of the vault where the sarcophagus lies!"
cried Rumphius, letting his light-gray eyes, that
sparkled with delight, be seen beneath his spectacles,
pushed up on his brow.

"So far," said Evandale, "the Greek has not
failed in his part of the bargain. We are indeed the
first human beings who have entered here since the
dead, whoever he may be, was abandoned to eternity
and oblivion in this tomb."

"Oh, he must have been a very powerful personage," replied the doctor; "a king, or a prince of the
royal household at least. I will tell you after I
decipher his cartouche. But first let us enter this
room, the most important and most beautiful of
all, and the one that the Egyptians called the *Golden
Room.*"

Lord Evandale moved on a little in advance of
the savant, who was less active, or who wanted to
yield, out of deference, the first rights of the discovery to the young nobleman.

3*

As he was about to cross the threshold, Lord Evandale leaned forward as if something unexpected met his glance. Although accustomed to mask his feelings,—as nothing is more opposed to the principles of dandyism in high circles than to betray your own inferiority upon any point by manifesting surprise or admiration,—the young lord could not suppress an " Oh !"—prolonged and modulated with true British emphasis.

This is what called forth an exclamation from one of the most accomplished gentlemen of the three united kingdoms : upon the fine gray powder covering the floor was a distinct print of the five toes and the heel of a human foot,—the foot of the last priest or the last friend who departed from this spot fifteen hundred years before the advent of Jesus Christ, after having paid the final honors to the dead. The dust, as lasting as the granite in Egypt, had moulded this footprint and preserved it for more than thirty centuries, as the hardened diluvian clay preserves the petrified tracks of animals.

" Look," said Evandale to Rumphius, " at this human footprint pointing towards the entrance of the tomb. Perhaps the embalmed remains of the one who made it are to be found now in some syrinx of this Libyan chain."

" Who knows ?" rejoined the savant. " At all events, this slight trace, that a breath of air might have blown away, has endured longer than races, empires, religions even, and monuments that were supposed to be eternal. The noble dust of Alexander, perhaps, is stopping the bung-hole of some beer-barrel, according to Hamlet's reflection, and the footprint of an obscure Egyptian is still to be found at the door-sill of a sepulchre!"

Urged on by a curiosity that would not permit lengthy reflections, the young nobleman and the doctor crossed the threshold, taking pains not to efface the wonderful footprint. Upon entering the room, the impassible Evandále experienced a singular sensation. It seemed to him, as Shakspeare expresses it, " that time was out of joint," and for the moment every idea of modern life vanished.

He forgot Great Britain and his name inscribed in the golden book of the nobility, his possessions in Lincolnshire, his mansions at West End, Hyde Park, and Piccadilly, the Queen's drawing-rooms, his club, and everything that constitutes an Englishman's existence. An invisible hand had reversed the hour-glass of eternity, and the centuries that had fallen grain by grain into silence and night recommenced their course. History became a thing of the present. Moses lived, Pharaoh reigned, and he, Lord Evandale, felt embarrassed because he did not have on an Egyptian head-dress, a necklace of enamels, and a narrow kilt about the loins,—the only costume in which he might present himself before a royal mummy.

A species of religious awe took possession of him —although there was nothing sinister about the place—at thus desecrating a palace of the dead so carefully protected against violators.

The attempt seemed to him wicked and sacrilegious, and he said to himself, " What if Pharaoh were to rise up from his couch and strike me with his sceptre?" For an instant he felt like letting the half-lifted veil fall again over the dead limbs of this relic of ancient civilization; but the doctor, full of the enthusiasm of science, had not stopped to reflect, and presently cried out, in ringing tones, " My lord, my lord, the sarcophagus is intact !"

This exclamation recalled Lord Evandale to reality. Like an electric flash, his thoughts flew back over the three thousand five hundred years of his revery, and he replied, " Is it possible, my dear doctor,—intact ?"

" An incredible good fortune ! A marvellous chance ! A priceless treasure !" continued the doctor, with scientific rapture.

Argyropoulos, seeing the enthusiasm of the doctor, felt a pang of remorse, the only kind of remorse he could ever experience,—that of not having demanded more than twenty-five thousand francs.

" I was foolish," he said to himself; "but it shall not happen a second time. This *milord* has robbed me." And he made a vow that he would be more careful in future.

The Arabs lighted all their torches, so that the strangers might take in the beauty of the scene at a glance. It was indeed a strange and magnificent spectacle! The galleries and apartments leading to the chamber of the sarcophagus had flat ceilings, not more than eight or ten feet in height; but the sanctuary where these labyrinths ended was of very different proportions. Lord Evandale and Rumphius were speechless with admiration, although already accustomed to the funeral splendors of Egyptian art.

The Golden Room was a blaze of light, and for the first time, perhaps, the colors of the paintings were exhibited in all their brilliance. Reds, blues, greens, whites, with a new lustre, a virgin freshness, an astonishing purity, stood out upon a coating of gold, serving as background to the figures and hieroglyphics, and attracted the eye before it could distinguish the subjects illustrated in their assemblage. At first sight it might have been taken for tapestry of the richest kind; the vaulted ceiling, thirty feet in height, was like a blue *velarium* edged with long yellow palm - branches. On the walls the symbolic globe spread its vast wings, and royal cartouches inscribed their ovals. Farther on, Isis and Nephthys stretched forth their feathered arms like birds' pinions. The uroei-snakes swelled their azure throats, the scarabæi tried to unfold their elytra, the gods, with the heads of animals, raised their jackal ears, stuck out their sparrow-hawk bills, puckered up their cynocephalous noses, and settled their vulture or serpent necks between their shoulders as if endued with life. Mystic funeral barges passed on sledges drawn by conventional figures in angular

c

positions, or, rowed by half-naked oarsmen, floated
upon a stream of water indicated by symmetrically-
waved lines. Mourners, kneeling with their hands
laid upon their blue locks to express their sorrow,
turned themselves towards catafalques, while priests,
with shaven heads, and leopard-skins thrown over
their shoulders, burned perfumes on the end of a
spatula terminating in a hand holding a little cup
under the noses of the sacred dead. Other personages offered to the divinities presiding over death
the lotus,—full-blown or in bud,—bulbous plants,
fowls, quarters of antelope, and vases of wine. The
headless justices brought in souls, with their arms
confined as if in strait-jackets, before Osiris, as-
sisted by the forty-two assessors of Amenti squatted
down in two files, and wearing upon their heads,
borrowed from every department of zoology, a fluttering ostrich-plume. All of these representations,
cut firmly in the chalk and dashed with brilliant
colors, had that immovable life, that congealed
movement, that mysterious intensity of Egyptian
art, under the restraints of priestly influence, that
makes one think of a man with a gag in his mouth
trying to divulge some secret.

In the centre of the room loomed up the massive
and imposing sarcophagus, hollowed out of an enormous block of black basalt, and covered with a
bevelled top of the same. The four sides of this
funeral monolith were covered with figures and
hieroglyphics, as finely engraved as the intaglio of a

valuable ring, although the Egyptians did not know the use of iron, and there is a refractory grain in basalt that dulls the edge of the hardest steel. One is put to his wits' end to know by what process this wonderful people wrote on porphyry and granite as though they were using a stylus on tablets of wax.

At the angles of the sarcophagus were deposited four vases of Oriental alabaster of the most elegant form, the sculptured lids of which represented Amset with the head of a man, the baboon-headed Hapi, Soumaoutf with the head of a jackal, and Kebsnif with that of a sparrow-hawk : these were the vases that held the viscera of the mummy contained in the sarcophagus. At the head of the tomb, as though keeping guard over the sleep of the dead, stood an effigy of Osiris with braided beard. Two painted statues of women stood either side of the monument, supporting a square box on the head with one hand, and a vase for libations on the hip with the other. One wore a simple white skirt, clinging to the figure, and held by crossed bretelles ; the other, more richly attired, limped along in a garment of red and green scales, fitting like a sheath. Beside the former were three jars, once filled with Nile water, that in evaporating had left nothing but a clay sediment, and a dish, containing the dried remains of some kind of food. Beside the latter stood two little ships, resembling the models of vessels made at seaports, one of them representing, in every detail, the boats destined for transporting the body from Diospolis to the Memnonia; the other, the symbolic barge that carried the soul to the regions of the Occident. Nothing was forgotten, neither masts, nor rudder, made of a long oar, nor pilot, nor oarsmen, nor the mummy, surrounded with mourners and lying beneath a canopy, on a bed with lions' feet, nor the allegorical figures of the funeral divinities accomplishing their sacred offices. Boats and individuals were depicted in vivid colors, and on the sides of the prow, bent upward like a beak, in the same manner as the stern, was the great Osirian eye, lengthened with antimony; a beef's skull and bones, scattered here and there, proved that some victim had been offered up to secure an undisturbed repose for the dead. Caskets painted and decked with hieroglyphics were laid upon the tomb; reed tables still held some funeral offerings; nothing had been touched in this palace of Death since the day when the mummy, in its coffins and cerements, had been laid upon its couch of basalt. Even the worm of the sepulchre, that knows so well how to make its way into the strongest casket, had retraced its course, repelled by the strong odors of bitumen and spices.

"Shall we open the sarcophagus?" asked Argyropoulos, after Lord Evandale and Rumphius had spent some time in admiring the splendors of the Golden Room.

"Certainly," replied the young lord; "but take care not to injure the corners of the lid in introducing your bars, for I want to remove this monument and make a present of it to the British Museum."

All of the party lent their aid in opening the monolith; wooden wedges were carefully inserted, and, after a few moments' labor, the enormous cover yielded and slid down upon the supports put there to receive it. The open sarcophagus disclosed to view the outer coffin, hermetically sealed. It was a box, ornamented with paintings and gilding, representing a sort of shrine, with elegant patterns in lozenges, squares, palm-branches, and rows of hieroglyphics. The cover was removed, and Rumphius, who was leaning over the sarcophagus, uttered a cry of amazement when he saw the contents of the coffin. "A woman! A woman!" he exclaimed, recognizing the sex of the mummy by the absence of the Osirian beard and the shape of the inner case. The Greek, too, seemed astonished: his long experience as excavator made him fully aware of all that was novel in this discovery.

The valley of Bibán-el-Molook is the Saint-Denis of ancient Thebes, and contains only the tombs of the kings. The necropolis of the queens is situated farther off, in a gorge of the mountains. The tombs of the queens are very simple, and have generally only two or three galleries and a corresponding number of chambers. The women of the East have always been considered inferior to the men even after death. The greater part of these tombs, violated at very remote epochs, have served as receptacles for deformed mummies, rudely embalmed, that still exhibit traces of leprosy and elephantiasis.

By what means, by what miracle or substitution, had this woman's coffin found its way into this royal sarcophagus, in the midst of this palatial crypt, worthy of the most illustrious and the most powerful of the Pharaohs?

"This unsettles all of my opinions and theories," said the doctor to Lord Evandale, "and contradicts the most reliable authorities on the subject of the Egyptian funeral rites, so uniform in every respect, however, for thousands of years! No doubt we have alighted upon some mystery, some obscure point lost to history. A woman once mounted the throne of the Pharaohs and governed Egypt. She was called Tahoser, if we are to believe the cartouches engraven upon the records of the most ancient inscriptions; she has usurped the tomb, as she did the throne, or perhaps some ambitious woman, whom history does not mention, imitated her example."

"No one is better fitted than yourself to decide the difficult question," said Lord Evandale. "Let us carry away this chestful of secrets to our boat, where you can examine the historical document at your ease, and I have no doubt that you will solve the enigmas of these sparrow-hawks, scarabæi, kneeling figures, serrated lines, urœi-serpents, and hands with spatulas, as readily as the great Champollion."

The fellahs, directed by Argyropoulos, took up the enormous coffin on their shoulders, and the

mummy, starting forth again, in an inverse sense,
upon the same funeral route over which it had
passed in the days of Moses, in a painted and gilded
barge, preceded by a long train, embarked upon the
sandal that had brought the travellers thither, soon
reached the dahabeëh anchored in the Nile, and was
placed in the cabin, that resembled somewhat, as
things change so little in Egypt, the temple in which
it had rested on the funeral barge. Argyropoulos,
having ranged about the coffin all the objects found
near it, stood respectfully at the door, as if waiting
for something. Lord Evandale understood, and
made his *valet-de-chambre* count him out twenty-
five thousand francs. The open coffin stood upon
supports in the middle of the cabin, shining as brilliantly as if colors and patterns had been laid on the
night before, and displaying in its frame the mummy,
enveloped in a case remarkable for its rich and
elaborate decoration. Never had old Egypt swathed
one of her children for its last sleep with greater
care. Although there was no outline of form in this
funereal Hermes, where shoulders and head alone
were indicated, it was evident that the thick covering
concealed a young and graceful figure. The gilded
mask, with long almond-shaped eyes, sparkling with
enamel, the nose with its delicately-cut nostrils, the
rounded cheeks, the full lips, wreathed with that
indescribable smile of the sphinx, the chin rather
short in its curve, but of an exquisite contour, presented the purest type of the ideal Egyptian, and

showed by a thousand little characteristic details that art does not invent the individual features of a portrait. A multitude of fine braids, plaited like cords, and separated by bandeaux, fell on each side of the mask in luxurious abundance. A branch of lotus, starting from the nape of the neck, encircled the upper part of the head, and opened its azure chalice upon the dead gold of the brow, completing, with the funeral cone, this rich and elegant coiffure. A wide collar of fine enamels inlaid with precious metal was thrown about the neck, revealing in its golden mould, between the descending rows, the firm, fair outlines of a youthful bust.

On the breast appeared the monstrous configuration, full of symbolic meaning, of the sacred bird with a ram's head, bearing between its green horns the red circle of the setting sun, and supported by two serpents, with bloated necks, wearing the pshent. Lower down in the spaces left free by transversal zones and striped with brilliant colors, representing *bandelettes*, the sparrow-hawk of Phré, crowned with a winged globe, the body covered with symmetrically-arranged feathers, and the tail spread like a fan, held between its claws the mysterious Tau, emblem of immortality. The funeral gods, with green faces and the muzzles of baboon and jackal, presented, with a hieratically rigid gesture, the scourge, the crook, and the sceptre; the Osirian eye dilated its red ball surrounded with antimony; the celestial vipers inflated their throats beneath the sacred disks; symbolical figures extended their feathered arms like threatening swords; and the two goddesses of the beginning and the end, stripped to the waist, with the rest of the body confined in a narrow skirt, and the hair strewn with blue powder, knelt, in the Egyptian posture, on green and red cushions ornamented with great tassels.

A longitudinal band, covered with hieroglyphics, starting from the waist, reached down to the feet, containing, no doubt, some formulas of the funeral ritual, or the name and titles of the deceased, a problem that Rumphius promised himself to resolve at a future date. From the style and design of these paintings, the boldness of drawing and vividness of coloring, it was evident to a practised eye that they belonged to the best period of Egyptian art. When the young lord and the savant had looked long enough at this first covering they drew the case from the box and set it up against the wall. It was a strange sight, this dead *maillot*, with its golden mask, standing there like a material phantom, and assuming again a false air of life, after having lain so long in a horizontal position on its bed of basalt, in the heart of a mountain laid bare by impious curiosity. The soul of the dead that had counted upon an eternal rest, and that had taken so much care to protect its mortal part from desecration, must have been troubled at this, in the other world, on its round of travels and metamorphoses.

Rumphius, armed with a chisel and a hammer to
4*

open the mummy-case, looked like one of the funeral
genii, in an animal mask, seen flocking about the
dead in the frescoes of the tomb, to accomplish some
mysterious and terrifying rite; Lord Evandale, attentive and calm, resembled, with his pure profile, the
divine Osiris, waiting to judge the soul, and, if one
desired to push the comparison still further, even
the stick in his hand suggested the sceptre of the
god.

The operation, which took some time, as the doctor
did not want to injure the gilding, being ended, the
box lay upon the ground, divided in two, like an open
mould, and the mummy appeared in all the splendor
of its funeral apparel, as coquettish in all its appoint-
ments as if it had wanted to captivate the spirits of
the subterranean world.

On opening the case, a vague and delicious odor of
spices, cedar-tree pitch, sandal-wood powder, myrrh,
and cassia diffused itself through the cabin of the
dahabeëh : for the body had not been saturated and
stiffened with the black bitumen that makes the
ordinary mummies so rigid, and all the art of the
embalmers, the ancient inhabitants of the Memnonia,
seemed to have been employed in trying to preserve
these precious remains.

Narrow bands of fine linen, interlaced, through
which the features were partly distinguishable, enveloped the head ; the spices with which they had been
impregnated had stained the material a beautiful fawn
color. A net-work of slender blue-glass tubes, like

the bits of jet used in embroidering Spanish bas-
quines, united at their points of intersection by tiny
gold beads, covered the linen armor, and, reaching
from the breast to the thighs, formed a jewelled shroud
worthy of a queen ; little figures of the four gods of
Amenti, in *repoussé* gold, gleamed in a symmetrical
row in the upper part of the net-work, which ended
below in an ornamental fringe of the most perfect
workmanship.

Between the figures of the funeral gods was a pen-
dant, consisting of a disk of gold, over which a scarabæus of lapis-lazuli spread its gilded wings. Under
the head of the mummy was placed a rich mirror of
polished metal, as if to furnish the soul of the deceased
with the means of contemplating the spectre of its
charms during the long night of death. Near the
mirror was a beautiful casket of enamelled ware, en-
closing a necklace made of rings of ivory and beads
of gold, lapis-lazuli, and cornelian. Beside the body
lay the narrow oblong bowl of sandal-wood in which,
during her lifetime, the dead had accomplished her
perfumed ablutions.

Three vases of veined alabaster, fastened like the
mummy to a bed of natron at the bottom of the coffin,
contained, two of them, ointments still retaining their
odor, and the other antimony powder, with a little
bodkin, for staining the eyelids and lengthening the
exterior angle, according to the ancient Egyptian
custom, still practised in our day by the women of
the Orient.

"What a touching custom," said **Dr. Rumphius**, enthusiastically, as he spied these treasures, "to bury a young woman with all the coquettish arsenal of her toilet about her! For there can be no doubt that it is a young woman enveloped in these bands of linen stained yellow with age and essences. Compared with the Egyptians, we are veritable barbarians: dragging out a mere animal existence, we no longer have any delicacy of sentiment connected with death. What tenderness, what regret, what love, are revealed in this devoted attention, this unlimited precaution, this vain solicitude that no one would ever witness, this affection lavished upon an insensible corpse, these efforts to snatch from destruction an adored form, and to present it to the soul intact upon the great day of the resurrection!"

"Perhaps," returned Lord Evandale, thoughtfully, "our civilization, that we consider superior to all others, is but a grand decadence, possessing no longer a historic recollection of the giant races of the past. We are stupidly proud of some ingenious mechanical contrivances of recent invention, and we do not take into account the colossal splendors, the magnificence beyond the reach of any other people but those of the land of Pharaoh. We have steam; but steam is not as powerful as the thought that raised the pyramids, excavated the tombs, cut mountains into sphinxes and obelisks, paved rooms with a single block that none of our engines could lift, formed chapels out of monoliths, and found means to defend the frail human body from annihilation, so well did it understand the meaning of eternity!"

"Oh, the Egyptians," said Rumphius, smiling, "were prodigious architects, wonderful artists, and profoundly-learned men. The priests of Memphis and Thebes could have given some points to our German savants, and in symbolism they were equal to several Creuzers; but some day we will comprehend their mysterious language and grasp their secrets. The great Champollion has furnished us with an alphabet; and as for the rest of us, we will soon read their books of granite fluently. In the mean time, let us disrobe this young beauty, more than three thousand years old, with all the delicacy possible."

"Poor lady!" murmured the young lord; "profane eyes are about to rest upon charms unknown to love itself, perhaps. Oh, yes, under the vain pretext of science, we are as savage as the Persians of Cambyses; and, if I were not afraid of causing this honest doctor chagrin, I would seal you up again, without removing the last veil, in the triple enclosure of your coffins!"

Rumphius, lifting from the cartonage the mummy, which weighed no more than a child, began to undo the wrappings with all the skill and care of a mother undressing her babe: he first unfastened the covering of stitched linen, soaked in palm-wine, and the wide bands encircling the body at intervals; then he found the end of a narrow band, surrounding the members of the young Egyptian in innumerable spirals, and rolled it up within itself, following all its windings and turnings as neatly as the most skilful tarichcute of the City of the Dead could have done it. As his work advanced, the mummy, losing its thickness, like the statue that the sculptor is hewing from a block of marble, grew more slender and shapely. This *bandelette* disposed of, another presented itself, still narrower, and intended to bind the form more closely. It was of linen so fine, and so admirably woven, that it would bear comparison with the muslin and batiste of our day. It followed the contours of the figure, carefully imprisoning fingers, hands, and feet, and moulding, as in a mask, the features of the face, already almost visible through the transparent texture. The essences with which it had been saturated had stiffened it, and in peeling off under the doctor's fingers it made a little rustling sound, like paper when it is crumpled or torn. A single round remained, and Dr. Rumphius, familiar as he was with such operations, ceased his labors for a moment, whether out of a species of respect for the dead, or for the same reason that prevents us from breaking the seal of a letter, opening a door, or lifting the veil that hides some secret we long to know. He accounted for this pause by saying that he was tired; and, in fact, the perspiration was streaming from his brow, without his ever thinking of the famous blue-checked handkerchief; but fatigue had nothing to do with it.

However, the dead was visible under the fine material as if it had been covered with gauze, and there was a faint glimmer of gilding through the threads.

The last obstacle removed, the young woman appeared in all the chaste nudity of her beautiful figure, retaining, in spite of so many centuries gone by, all that roundness of contour, all that supple grace of perfect lines. Her pose, unusual with mummies, was that of Venus de' Medici, as though the embalmers had sought to remove the sorrowful attitude of death from this fair form and divest it of the inflexible rigidity of the corpse, and as if the modesty of the dead had even trembled for itself amid the protecting shadows of the tomb.

A cry of admiration burst simultaneously from the lips of Rumphius and Evandale at sight of this wonder. Never had Greek or Roman statue presented a more elegant type; the particular characteristics of the Egyptian ideal gave to this beautiful form, so miraculously preserved, a slenderness and litheness that antique marbles do not possess. The slight tapering fingers, with nails brilliant as agate, the high-bred narrow feet, the slender waist, the small bust, showing its firm, beautiful outlines beneath the gold-leaf covering, the contour of the hip not too prominent, the roundness of the thigh, the leg a little long, with delicately-moulded ankles, recalling the pliant grace of the musicians and dancers, represented in the frescoes, assisting at the funeral banquets in the sepulchres at Thebes. It is this form, still retaining the grace of the child with the perfections of the woman, that Egyptian art portrays with such tender suavity, whether it be painted upon the walls of a syrinx with rapid brush, or patiently carved in the stubborn basalt. Ordinarily mummies prepared with bitumen and natron resemble black images cut out of ebony; dissolution cannot approach them, but all appearance of life is gone. The corpse has not returned to the dust from whence it came, but it has hardened into a repulsive object, impossible to contemplate without a feeling of disgust and horror. Here the body, prepared by a longer, safer, and more costly process, had preserved the elasticity of the flesh, the grain of the epidermis, and a color that was almost natural; the skin, of a light brown, had the fine hue of a new Florentine bronze; and the warm amber tint, so much admired in the paintings of Giorgione and Titian, grown mellow under the varnish, could not have differed much from that of the young Egyptian when alive.

The features wore the calm of slumber more than that of death; the eyelids, fringed with long lashes, showed between their edges, stained with antimony, the enamel of the eyes, lustrous with the dewy light of life; it seemed as if they were about to shake off, like the dream of a moment, the sleep of thirty centuries. The nose, small and delicate, had retained its pure outlines; no depression deformed the beautiful oval of the cheeks; the mouth tinged with

a faint color was gently closed; and on the volup-
tuously-modelled lips rested a melancholy and mysterious smile, charmingly sweet and sad: the same
smile that closes, in such a delicious curve, the
mouths of those adorable heads surmounting the
Canopian vases in the Louvre.

About the brow, level and low, in accordance with
the laws of antique beauty, were massed the jet-black
tresses, divided into a multitude of fine cord-like
plaits, that fell on either shoulder.

Twenty golden hair-pins, thrust in among the
locks like flowers in a ball-coiffure, gleamed like
stars in the thick dark hair, so abundant that one
might have thought it was false.

Two large ear-rings, round disks like tiny shields,
hung trembling with a yellow light against the brown
cheeks.

A superb necklace, made of three rows of divinities and amulets in gold and precious stones, encircled the neck of the coquettish mummy, and lower
down upon the breast lay two other necklaces, whose
beads and rosettes of gold, lapis-lazuli, and cornelian
were combined with exquisite taste. A girdle of a
similar design clasped the slender waist with a circle
of gold and precious stones. A bracelet, with double
rows of gold and cornelian beads, surrounded the
left wrist, and on the index finger of the same hand
sparked a tiny scarabæus, made of enamels veined
with gold and secured to the collet of the ring by a
finely-wrought golden wire.

What a strange sensation ! to find one's self face to face with a human being that had lived at a period when history was in its infancy, collecting traditional accounts in the presence of a beauty contemporaneous with Moses and still preserving the lovely features of youth; to take up that dainty little hand, impregnated with perfumes, that perhaps a Pharaoh had kissed; to touch those braids more durable than empires, more lasting than monuments of granite !

As he stood beside the dead beauty, the young lord experienced that retrospective longing often inspired by the sight of a marble or a painting representing a woman of past time celebrated for her charms : it seemed to him that he might have loved her if he had lived three thousand five hundred years ago, this fair being that the grave had left untouched, and his feeling of sympathy may have attained the anxious soul, hovering near the profaned remains.

Far less poetic than the young lord, Dr. Rumphius proceeded to make an inventory of the jewels without removing them, as Evandale had desired that this last poor consolation should not be removed from the mummy,—to take away her jewels from a woman after death would be to kill her a second time !—when all at once a roll of papyrus, hidden beneath the arm of the mummy, attracted his eyes.

"Ah !" said he, "no doubt it is a copy of the funeral ritual that they put in the last coffin, written with more or less care, according to the wealth and importance of the individual."

And he began to undo the fragile roll with the greatest care. On glancing at the first lines, Rumphius seemed surprised; he did not recognize the ordinary signs and symbols of the ritual; he sought in vain, in the usual place, for the vignettes representing the funeral and its cortège, that serve as frontispiece to this papyrus; neither could he find the litany of the hundred names of Osiris, nor the passport of the soul, nor the supplications addressed to the four gods of Amenti. Drawings of a certain kind showed different scenes connected with life on earth, instead of the dark journey into the world beyond.

Chapters, or parts, seemed to be indicated by characters traced in red, to distinguish them from the rest of the text, done in black, and to draw the attention of the reader to the most important parts.

An inscription placed at the top apparently contained the title of the work and the name of the scribe who had written it or made the copy; at least this seemed probable to the shrewd mind of the doctor at first sight.

"Decidedly, my lord, we have robbed *le sieur* Argyropoulos," said Rumphius to Evandale, directing his attention to all the points of difference between this papyrus and the ordinary rituals. "It is the first time that an Egyptian manuscript has been found containing anything but the hieratic formulas. Oh, I will decipher it, if I put out my eyes in the

attempt and my untrimmed beard reaches three
times around my writing-table! Yes, I will wrest
your secret from you, mysterious Egypt! yes, I will
learn your history, dead beauty, for this papyrus,
pressed against your heart by your lovely arm,
must contain it! And I will cover myself with
glory, equal Champollion, and make Lepsius die of
jealousy!"

The doctor and the young lord returned to Europe; the mummy, enveloped anew in its bandages,
lies in its three coffins in Lord Evandale's park in
Lincolnshire, within the sarcophagus of basalt that
he had sent on at a great expense from Bibán-el-
Molook and did not present to the British Museum.
Sometimes the young nobleman comes and leans
against the sarcophagus, seems lost in a profound
revery, and sighs.

After three years of persevering study, Rumphius
managed to decipher the mysterious papyrus, except
in a few instances where corrections had been made
or unknown characters appeared, and it is his Latin
translation that we have anglicized from the French
for your perusal under the following title: "The
Romance of a Mummy."

CHAPTER I.

OPH—for this was the Egyptian name of the town known to antiquity as Thebes with a hundred gates, or Diospolis Magna—seemed to have fallen asleep under the scorching rays of a sun of lead. It was noon; a blanched light fell from the pallid sky to the drooping earth; the sun, flashing from every point, gleamed like burnished metal, and there was only a bluish thread of shadow at the foot of the buildings, resembling the line of ink with which the architect traces his plan on papyrus; the slightly-sloping walls of the houses glowed like bricks in a furnace; the doors were closed, and not a head was to be seen at the windows, shielded by blinds of plaited reeds.

At the ends of the deserted streets and above the terraces stood out in relief, in an atmosphere of in-candescent purity, the points of the obelisks, the summits of the pylons, and the entablatures of the palaces and temples, whose capitals, showing glimpses of human faces and lotus-flowers, interrupted the straight line of the roofs, and rose one above the other like shelves in this assemblage of private dwellings.

Here and there, above some garden-wall, a palm-tree sent up its laminated shaft, ending in a fan-like

5*

bunch of leaves, every one of which was motionless, for there was not a breath to ruffle the atmosphere; cascades of foliage fell from acacias, Pharaoh's fig-trees, and mimosas, tingeing the glistening surface of the ground with a scarcely perceptible blue shadow. These dashes of green enlivened and refreshed the dreary aridity of the picture, that, but for them, would have presented the aspect of a dead city.

Some rare black slaves of the Nahasi race, with the head of a monkey and an animal's gait, braving alone the heat of the day, bore to their masters water drawn from the Nile in jars suspended from a stick resting upon the shoulders. Although their sole garment consisted of a pair of short striped drawers, their bodies, polished and bright as black marble, streamed with perspiration, and they quickened their steps so as not to burn the thick soles of their feet on the paving-stones, hot as the floor of an oven.

The boatmen slept under the canopies of their boats, moored to the brick quay of the river, confident that no one would awaken them to pass over to the other shore in the quarter of the Memnonia. Far up in the heavens hawks were flying to and fro, the general silence making audible their shrill notes, that at any other time of the day would have been lost in the tumult of the city.

The slim silhouettes of two or three ibises, standing upon the cornices of the monuments on one leg, with their beaks buried in their breasts as if in profound meditation, were sharply defined upon the calcined and colorless blue of the background.

However, all Thebes was not sleeping: from the walls of a grand palace, whose entablature, adorned with palm-leaves, stood out in a long horizontal line against the burning sky, issued vague and subdued musical tones. These harmonious utterances were borne from time to time through the tremulous purity of the atmosphere, where it seemed almost as if the eye could follow the waves of sound. Muffled by the thick intervening walls as by a *sourdine*, the music was strangely sweet; it was a song of a voluptuous plaintiveness, of a tired languor, express-ing weariness of the body and the sorrows of love, and suggestive of the luminous ennui of eternal blue skies and the indefinable depression of hot climes.

As he passed this wall, the slave, forgetful of his master's whip, stayed his steps to listen with an attentive ear to this song, impregnated with the secret nostalgia of the soul, that recalled his native land, his sundered affections, and all the insurmount-able obstacles of fate.

Whence came this song, this sigh breathing itself out in the silence of the city? What restless soul watched while all was sleeping around it?

The façade of the palace, fronting upon a rather large square, had the severity of line and the monu-mental appearance that characterize Egyptian archi-tecture, whether civil or religious.

This dwelling could be none other than that of a princely or sacerdotal household, it was evident from the choice of materials, the finish of the building, and the wealth of ornamentation.

In the centre of the façade rose a great pavilion, with two wings, surmounted by a roof forming a depressed triangle. A wide and very concave mould-ing, presenting a sharp profile, finished the wall, in which there was no opening to be seen except a door, not placed symmetrically in the middle, but in one corner of the pavilion,—probably so as not to inter-fere with the bend of an interior staircase.

A cornice, in the same style as the entablature, crowned this single entrance.

The pavilion projected from a wall, to which were attached, as balconies, two-storied galleries or open porches, with columns of a singularly fantastic struc-ture: the vases represented immense lotus-buds, and the shafts shot up between the jagged edges of the calyx like gigantic pistils, swelling below and spin-dling above, till, clasped in the embrace of the capi-tals, as in a necklace of mouldings, they expanded in the full-blown flower.

In the wide spaces between the pillars, small win-dows with folding valves, containing stained glass, were visible; overhead was a terrace paved with enormous flags.

Great earthen jars, rubbed on the inside with bitter almonds and their mouths filled with leaves, were placed on wooden tripods in these galleries for the purpose of keeping the Nile water fresh in the currents of air.

Tables stood there also, bearing pyramids of fruits, sheaves of flowers, and drinking-cups of various shapes,—for the Egyptians loved to eat in the open air and take their repast, so to speak, on the public highways.

On either side of this portico were buildings of a single story, consisting of a row of columns half embedded in a panelled wall, or dado, extending to nearly half their height, and forming a promenade around the house protected from the sun and prying eyes. All of this architecture, enlivened with ornamental painting,—for capitals, shafts, cornices, and panels were colored,—produced an effect both pleasing and gorgeous. Passing through the doorway, you entered upon a vast court surrounded by a quadrilateral porch, supported by pillars having at their capitals four female heads with the ears of a cow, long oval eyes, slightly-flattened noses, and full smiling lips, framed in thick striped hoods surmounted by cones of hard sandstone.

Within this porch were doors leading to apartments where the only light that entered was softened by the shade of the gallery.

In the midst of the court, sparkling in the sunlight, was an artificial pond surrounded by a border of Syene granite, and on its surface lay the great heart-shaped leaves of the lotus, whose pink and blue flowers were half shut, as though overcome with the heat, in spite of the water in which they were floating.

In the plat-bands framing the tank were flowers planted in fan-shaped rows on little hills of earth, and in the narrow paths between the beds were two tame swans, carefully picking their way along, now and then bringing their long bills together with a clap and fluttering their wings as if they wanted to fly away.

At the angles of the court, four large perseas with twisted trunks spread their masses of metallic green foliage.

In the background a sort of pylon was set in the porch, showing in the blue space beyond, at the end of a long vine-covered bower, a summer-house of a rich and elegant design.

The compartments, divided off right and left of the arbor by dwarf trees trimmed in the shape of cones, were full of the verdure of sycamores, tamarisks, periplocas, pomegranates, mimosas, and acacias, whose blossoms gleamed like showers of colored sparks against the dense background of foliage towering above the wall. The faint, sweet music we have spoken of proceeded from one of the chambers whose doors opened upon the inner porch.

Although the sun shone full into the court, flooding the ground with strong light till it glistened, a cool blue shadow, transparent in its intensity, filled the apartment, in the midst of which the eye, blinded by the glare outside, was unable at first to distin-

guish objects, but finally succeeded in making them
out as it became accustomed to the obscurity.

The walls of the room were tinted a delicate lilac,
and the cornice was bedecked with brilliant colors
and gold palm-leaves. The architectural divisions,
happily combined, exhibited on the flat surfaces
panels containing designs, ornaments, flower-sheaves,
figures of birds, checker-work in contrasting colors,
and scenes from private life.

In the background stood a bed of an odd form,
representing an ox, wearing ostrich plumes upon its
head and a disk between the horns, the back flattened out to receive those in search of repose upon
the narrow crimson mattress, the black legs with
green hoofs planted upon the floor as supports, and
the forked tail held erect. This quadruped-couch,
this piece of animal-furniture, would have seemed
strange in any other land but Egypt, where lions
and jackals alike were turned into beds at the caprice
of the cabinet-maker.

An *escabeau* with four steps, for the purpose of
mounting the bed, stood at its side, and at the head
was placed a crescent-shaped pillow of Oriental alabaster, intended to support the neck without disar-
ranging the hair.

In the centre there was a table of costly wood
and fine workmanship, its circular top resting upon
a fluted pedestal.

It was strewn with divers articles: a vase of
lotus-flowers, a mirror of polished bronze with an

ivory handle, a jar of veined alabaster full of antimony powder, and a long shallow box, carved from
sycamore wood, and representing a maiden, stripped
to the waist, in the act of swimming, and holding
above the water a spatula for perfumes.

Near the table, in a graceful attitude of nonchalance and melancholy, a young woman, or rather
a young girl, of marvellous beauty, was reclining
in a fauteuil of gilded wood, enlivened by touches
of red, with blue legs, arms shaped like lions, and
a thick cushion rolling over the top, of a purple
ground, flecked with gold and checkered with black
lines.

Her features, of an ideal delicacy, belonged to the
purest Egyptian type, and the sculptors must often
have had her in mind, even at the risk of infringing
the severe hieratic laws, when carving the images of
Isis and Hathor; gold and roseate reflections tinged
the warm pallor framing the dark almond-shaped
eyes, elongated with antimony, and full of an un-
speakable sadness. These large sombre eyes, with
straight dark brows and stained lids, had a strange
air in the lovely, almost childlike face. The half-
open mouth, of the hue of a pomegranate flower,
disclosed a line of liquid pearls between the full lips,
on which rested the involuntary and almost mournful smile that lends such a sympathetic charm to
Egyptian faces; the nose, slightly depressed at the
point of juncture where the eyebrows melted together
in a velvety shade, rose in such pure lines, the pro-

portions were so delicate, and the nostrils so finely chiselled, that any woman or goddess might have been satisfied with it, even though the profile was almost imperceptibly African; the beautifully-moulded chin had the polish of ivory; the cheeks, a little rounder than among other races, lent to this physiognomy an expression of sweetness and grace exceedingly charming.

This beautiful girl wore a head-dress simulating a guinea-fowl, the half-spread wings shading the temples, the pretty, slender head resting in the middle of the forehead, and the tail, dotted with white, covering the nape of the neck. An artful combination of enamels imitated the ocellated plumage of the bird well enough to deceive the eye; ostrich plumes, set in the casque like an aigrette, completed this head-dress reserved for young girls, in the same manner that the vulture, symbol of maternity, belonged exclusively to women. The brilliant black hair of the maiden hung in clusters of fine braids either side of the round smooth cheeks, bringing their contour into relief, and extending down to the shoulders; in their midst, like suns shining through a cloud, were ear-rings, in the form of immense gold hoops; two long fringed bands, attached to the head-dress, fell gracefully down the back.

A wide gorget, composed of several rows of enamels, gold and cornelian beads, fish and lizards in stamped gold, covered the breast from the throat to the bust, whose warm life-tints appeared through the transparent tissue of the *calasiris*.* The robe, showing wide cross-bars in the pattern, was confined at the waist by means of a sash with flowing ends, and trimmed at the bottom with a wide striped border, edged with a fringe.

Triple bracelets of lapis-lazuli beads, separated here and there by rows of gold beads, encircled the slender wrists, delicate as those of a child; and the pretty narrow feet, with long supple toes, shod in *tarbebs* of white leather embossed with gold, rested upon a stool of cedar incrusted with red and green enamels.

Near Tahoser (this was the name of the young Egyptian), with one knee bent under her and the other forming an obtuse angle, in the attitude that the artists loved to reproduce upon the walls of the tombs, was a harp-player, mounted upon a low pedestal, no doubt for the purpose of increasing the resonance of the instrument. A piece of stuff with colored stripes, the fluted ends of which, containing the hair, were thrown back, framed the face, smiling and mystic as that of a sphinx. A clinging dress, or rather a sheath of transparent gauze, moulded faithfully the juvenile contours of the slight and elegant form; this garment, cut away below the bust, left the shoulders, chest, and arms free in all their shapely nudity. A support set in the pedestal on which the musician was placed had a key-shaped peg attached to it, serving as *point d'appui* to the

---

* *Calasiris*, a long linen garment worn by the Egyptians.

harp, that without this would have leaned with its entire weight upon the shoulder of the young woman. The harp terminated in a species of sounding-board, rounded like a conch, and covered with ornamental painting, having at the upper end a head of Hathor, with an ostrich plume; the nine strings were stretched across it diagonally, and vibrated beneath the long adept fingers of the harper, who, in order to reach the lower notes, often leaned forward with a graceful motion, as if swaying to the sounding waves of harmony and seeking to follow them as they died away.

Behind her another musician, whom one might have fancied naked but for the mist of white drapery softening the bronze hue of her skin, stood playing a sort of mandora with a very long neck, whose three strings terminated in colored tassels. One of her arms, extended in a sculptural pose, supported the handle, while the other held the instrument and touched the strings.

A third young woman, whose very luxuriant hair made her appear even more reed-like, marked the time on a tambourine made of a wooden frame, bent in a little and covered with onager-skin.

The performer on the harp was singing a plaintive air, exceedingly sweet and sad, which she accompanied in unison. The words expressed vague longings, secret regrets, love for some unknown one, and timid laments because of the severity of the gods and the cruelty of fate.

Tahoser, with her elbow leaning on one of the lions of the fauteuil, her hand against her cheek and one finger touching the temple, listened to the song of the musician with a distraction more assumed than real; now and then a sigh swelled her bosom, lifting the enamels of her wide collar; or a liquid light, caused by a starting tear, made her eyes glisten between the dark lines of antimony, and she bit her under lip with her little teeth, as if endeavoring to control her feelings.

"Satou," said she, striking one delicate hand against the other to impose silence upon the musician, who stopped the vibrations of the strings at once with the palm of her hand, "your song saddens and enervates me. I feel as dizzy as though I had been inhaling too strong a perfume. The strings of your harp seem as if they were wound about the fibres of my heart, and their vibrations are painful to me; you almost put me to shame, for it is my own soul weeping in your music; and who could have told you its secrets?"

"Mistress," replied the harper, "the poet and the musician know all things; the gods reveal secrets to them, and they express in their rhythms that which the thought scarcely grasps, and which the tongue is powerless to utter. But if my song makes you sad, I can, by changing the movement, fill your mind with brighter thoughts."

And Satou struck the chords of her harp with a joyous energy to a lively air, accompanied by the quick beats of the tambourine; after this prelude she began a song praising the charms of wine, the intoxication of perfumes, and the delights of the dance.

Some of the women, who, under the depressing influence of Satou's music, had fallen into positions of hopeless languor, as they sat on camp-stools supported by the blue throats of swans grasping the rounds in their yellow beaks, or knelt on scarlet cushions stuffed with thistle-down, thrilled now through every nerve, distended their nostrils as if they wanted to breathe the magic rhythm into their being, rose to their feet, and, moved by an irresistible impulse, began to dance.

A head-covering in the shape of a helmet, cut away about the ear, confined the hair, a few curls of which, escaping, played over the brown cheeks, beginning to flush with the excitement of dancing. Immense hoops of gold swung against their throats, and through the long garment of gauze, embroidered about the neck with beads, their bodies, of a golden-bronze color, were visible, gliding to and fro with the suppleness of a lizard; they swayed like reeds, twirled themselves to and fro from the hips encircled by narrow girdles, leaned backwards, then poised themselves like a butterfly hovering over a flower, inclined the head first to the right and then to the left as if they found a secret pleasure in brushing their cool bare shoulders with their polished chins, bridled like doves, knelt and rose again lightly, pressed their hands against their chests, waved their arms about languidly as if they had plumes depending from them like those of Isis and Nephthys, trailed their limbs after them, bent the knee, and, lifting one foot after the other, beat the floor with quick staccato movements, keeping perfect time to the rhythmic flow of the music.

The attendants, standing against the wall so as to make room for the movements of the dancers, marked the time by snapping their fingers, or striking the palms of their hands together.

Some of them had no garments on, and no ornament but a bracelet of enamelled ware; the others were clad in narrow skirts supported by bretelles, and had wreaths of flowers twined among their locks. It was a strange and graceful spectacle. The buds and blossoms gently shaken diffused their perfume through the room, and these women with chaplets of flowers upon their heads might have offered happy subjects of comparison to the poet.

But Satou had overestimated the power of her art. The joyous air only seemed to increase the melancholy of Tahoser. A tear rolled down her beautiful cheek like a clear drop of Nile water over the petal of a nymphæa, and hiding her face on the shoulder of her favorite attendant, who was leaning with her arm upon the fauteuil of her mistress, she murmured, in a voice choked with sobs, "Oh, my dear Nofré, I am so sad and so unhappy!"

CHAPTER II.

NOFRÉ, believing that she wished to unburden her mind, made a sign to the harper, the two musicians, the dancers, and the other women, who retired silently in single file, like the figures in the fresco-paintings.

When the last one had disappeared, the favorite waiting-maid said to her mistress, in a coaxing and sympathetic tone of voice, as if she were a young mother trying to comfort her baby grieving over some trifle,—

"Why are you so sad and so unhappy, dear mistress? Do you not know that you are beautiful enough to make the fairest woman envious? Are you not free, and have you not inherited from your father, the great priest, Petamounoph, whose mummy lies hidden in a rich sepulchre, an immense fortune that you can do with as you like? Your palace is elegant, your vast gardens are well watered with refreshing streams. Your caskets of enamelled ware and sycamore wood contain collars, necklaces, anklets, and costly rings; your robes, calasireis, and head-dresses outnumber the days of the year; Hopi-Mou, the father of waters, never fails to irrigate your domains, whose extent a hawk could scarcely measure with its rapid flight from the dawn of one day to the sunset of the next; and yet your heart, instead of expanding joyfully, like the lotus-buds in the month of Hathor or Choïack, to the pleasure of existence, droops and mourns."

"Yes," responded Tahoser, "it is true that the gods who dwell above have shown me great favor; but what difference does it make how much we have, if the only thing we care for is lacking? An unsatisfied desire makes the rich man in his painted and gilded palace, surrounded by his grain, his spices, and various treasures, as poor as the most miserable workman of the Memnonia who removes the sawdust saturated with the blood of the dead, or the half-naked negro who paddles his frail bark of papyrus along the Nile under the scorching rays of the noonday sun."

Nofré smiled, and said, with a scarcely-perceptible air of raillery,—

"Have you ever expressed a desire, O my mistress, that was not gratified on the spot? If you are longing for an ornament, you have only to give the jeweller an ingot of pure gold, some lapis-lazuli and cornelian, some agates and hematites, and he will execute the design you want; it is the same with regard to your robes, your chariots, perfumes, flowers, and musical instruments. Your slaves go from Philæ to Heliopolis, searching for the rarest and most beautiful objects for you; and then if the coveted article is not to be found in Egypt, the caravans are here to bring it to you from the other end of the world!"

The beautiful Tahoser shook her pretty head, and seemed annoyed at her confidante's want of intelligence.

"Pardon, mistress," said Nofré, making another effort, as she perceived that she was on the wrong track, "I had forgotten that it is almost four months since Pharaoh started out on an expedition into Upper Ethiopia, and that the gallant *oëris* [officer], who never passed under your terrace without looking up and slackening his steps, accompanied his majesty. How well he looks in his uniform! How handsome, how young and brave he is!"

The scarlet lips of Tahoser parted as if she were going to speak, but a faint blush tinged her cheeks, she bent her head, and the phrase she was about to utter silently folded its wings. The attendant, believing that she was right in her conjectures, continued,—

"In that case, mistress, your troubles will soon end. This morning a breathless messenger arrived, announcing the triumphal return of the king before sunset. Do you not hear already the tumult and bustle outside in the city, which is awaking from its mid-day torpor? Listen! the wheels of the chariots are rattling over the paving-stones, and the people are hastening in crowds towards the shore of the river to cross over to the parade-ground. Shake off this languor, and let us go also to see the grand spectacle. When one is sad they must mingle with the crowd. Solitude fosters gloomy ideas. Ahmosis will smile graciously upon you from his war-chariot, and you will come back again to your palace with a light heart."

"Ahmosis loves me," replied Tahoser; "but I do not care for him."

"A young girl's speech," rejoined Nofré, who admired the handsome young warrior exceedingly, and who believed that Tahoser's disdainful nonchalance was feigned. In fact, Ahmosis was charming: his profile resembling the images of the gods fashioned by the best sculptors, his proud and regular features as beautiful as those of a woman, his nose slightly aquiline, his eyes of a brilliant black, enlarged with antimony, his smooth cheeks, of as fine a grain as Oriental alabaster, his well-shaped mouth, his tall and elegant figure, broad shoulders, slim waist, and powerful arms, no muscle of which, however, was rudely prominent, had every element of attraction even for the most fastidious; but Tahoser did not love him, whatever Nofré may have thought to the contrary. Another idea, which she did not disclose, because she thought Nofré incapable of understanding it, decided the young girl: she put aside her nonchalance, rose from her fauteuil with a vivacity that one would scarcely have expected of her, had they seen her drooping attitude in the midst of the music and the dancing. Nofré, kneeling beside her, placed upon her feet a pair of sandals, with the ends turned up like skates, threw perfumed powder upon her hair, took some bracelets in the shape of serpents and some rings mounted with scarabæi from a box, polished her nails with a preparation, touched her cheeks with a green cosmetic that changed to a rose-color on coming in contact with the skin, rearranged the slightly rumpled folds of her calasiris, like a devoted maid who wants her mistress to appear to the best advantage, then she summoned two or three servants, and ordered them to prepare the boat and transport the chariot and oxen to the other side of the river.

The palace, or, if this seems too grand a name, the mansion of Tahoser was situated upon the Nile, and only separated from it by the gardens. The daughter of Petamounoph, her hand resting upon Nofré's shoulder, and preceded by her servants, went down to the gate opening on the river, under the arbor, the vines, with the sunbeams sifting through them, flecking her charming face with light and shade.

She soon reached the large brick quay, swarming with an immense crowd awaiting the departure and return of the boats.

The heart of Oph, the colossal city, was emptied of all but invalids, infirm people, the aged who were unable to move, and the slaves who had charge of the houses: a tide of human beings was hastening through the streets, the squares, the dromos, the avenues of sphinxes, the pylons, and over the quays, towards the Nile. It was a very strange and motley assemblage: the majority were Egyptians, recognizable by their pure profiles, their tall, slender figures,

their robes of fine linen, or the carefully-pleated calasireis; and again by the head-dresses of striped stuff,
blue or green, the narrow kilts about the bodies, the
color of baked clay, naked to the belt.

Standing out in strong contrast against this background of natives were various specimens of foreign
races: negroes from the upper regions of the Nile,
black as idols carved from basalt, large ivory rings
on their arms, and savage ornaments swinging from
their ears; bronzed Ethiopians, with a wild air, as
uneasy, in spite of themselves, in the midst of this
civilization, as a beast of the forest would be roam-
ing about in daylight; Asiatics, with their light-
yellow skins, blue eyes, and beards hanging in curls,
attired in fringed robes, heavily embroidered, and
wearing tiaras attached to a band upon their heads;
and Pelasgians, clad in the skins of animals, fastened
at the shoulder and exposing to view their curiously-
tattooed limbs, while feathers adorned their heads,
from which hung two braids, ending in a lock
arranged in a flat curl.

Marching through the crowd, with a stately step,
were priests with shaven heads, draped with panther-
skins in such a manner as to make the head of the
animal appear like the buckle of a girdle, *byblus* sandals on their feet, and long walking-sticks of acacia,
engraved with hieroglyphics, in their hands; soldiers
with silver-studded poniards at their sides, shields
slung on their backs, and bronze hatchets in their
grasp; and persons of note, decorated with honorary

collars, before whom the slaves bowed low, almost touching the ground with their hands.

Keeping close to the walls, as they moved onward with a meek and mournful air, were some poor half-naked women, bending under the weight of their children, suspended from their shoulders by bits of ragged stuff or panniers of rush matting; while beautiful girls, accompanied by three or four servants, passed by with a haughty mien, in their long transparent robes, confined at the waist with a flowing sash, ablaze with jewels and enamels, and shedding an aroma of flowers and perfumes through the air.

Among the pedestrians might be seen litters borne by Ethiopians with a quick measured tread, light vehicles harnessed to spirited horses with nodding plumes, and family chariots drawn by slow-paced oxen.

The crowd, heedless of the danger of being crushed, scarcely opened to make room for them, and often the drivers were obliged to strike the headstrong and the laggards, who would not move out of the way, with their whips.

There was an unusual stir upon the river, covered, in spite of its breadth, with barks of every description, so that the water was scarcely visible from one end of the town to the other: everything navigable was in use, from the barge, with upturned prow and stern, and cabin resplendent with paint and gilding, to the tiniest shell of papyrus. Even the boats for the transportation of cattle and fruits, and the reed rafts buoyed on leather bottles, generally laden with earthenware jars, were not despised. It was not an easy matter to transfer a population of a million from one shore to the other, and to accomplish this it required all of the ready skill of the boatmen of Thebes.

The water of the Nile, beaten, whipped, and cut by paddles, oars, and rudders, foamed like a sea, and formed countless eddies that broke the force of the currents.

The structure of the boats was as varied as picturesque: some terminated at either end in a great lotus-flower, bent inward, with a streamer fastened to the stem; others had bifurcated sterns running to a point; one kind rounded like a crescent, turning up at both ends; another had a house or platform where the pilot stood; and some were made of three strips of bark bound together with thongs and propelled by a paddle. Boats intended for the transportation of animals and vehicles were placed side by side, and supported a flooring upon which was constructed a flying-bridge that simplified the work of embarking and disembarking; there was a great number of them.

The astonished horses neighed and struck the wood with their sounding hoofs; the oxen turned their lustrous muzzles, from which the foam was hanging in filaments, anxiously towards the shore, but grew calm again under the caressing touch of the leaders.

The boatswains marked the time for the rowers by clapping their hands; the pilots, standing at the stern or pacing the roof of the cabin, shouted their orders, indicating the manœuvres necessary for making headway in the midst of this confusion of crafts. Sometimes, in spite of every precaution, the boats collided, and the sailors exchanged insults, or struck each other with their oars.

These myriads of vessels, the greater part of them painted white and relieved by touches of blue, green, or red, crowded with men and women clad in garments of every hue, completely hid the surface of the Nile for several leagues, and, under the fiery rays of the Egyptian sun, presented a spectacle that was dazzling in its changes: the water, agitated on all sides, ran about as if it were made of quicksilver, turning every ripple into a burnished mirror, and making the whole surface look like a sun shivered into countless atoms.

Tahoser entered her superbly-decorated *cangia*,* in the centre of which stood a cabin, or *naos*, the entablature surmounted by a row of urœi-serpents, pillars supporting the corners, and the sides covered with a variety of admirable designs. A binnacle with a pointed roof occupied the stern, and a species of altar, decorated with brilliant colors, stood at the bow. The rudder was formed of two immense oars, ending at the top in the head of Hathor, tied about

---

* *Cangia*, a masted rowing-boat.

the neck with long streamers, and traversing upon a short pillar.

Flapping at the mast, for the wind had risen, was an oblong sail fastened to the yards. It was made of a rich material, gorgeously painted and embroidered in lozenge-shaped patterns, checker-work, birds, and fabulous animals, and large tassels hung from the lower yard.

The rope untied and the sail unfurled to the wind, the cangia left the shore, making a path with its prow through the mass of boats, whose oars became entangled and wriggled about helplessly like the legs of a scarabæus turned on its back. It moved onward calmly amid a chorus of invectives and shouts, its weight preventing it from feeling shocks that would have upset a lighter craft. On the other hand, the sailors of Tahoser were so skilful that the cangia they were managing seemed endued with intelligence itself, it obeyed the helm so promptly and avoided every dangerous obstacle.

It soon left in its wake the heavily-laden boats whose cabins were crowded with passengers inside, while three or four rows of men, women, and children were ranged upon the roof in the favorite Egyptian posture. To see these people kneeling thus, one might have taken them for the assessors of Osiris had their faces not been animated with an unmistakable gayety, instead of wearing a gravity suited to the counsellors of the Court of Death. For was not Pharaoh returning in triumph and

bringing with him a tremendous booty? Thebes
was rejoicing, and its entire population was on its way
to meet the beloved of Amon-Ra, lord of diadems,
president of the assemblies,—Aroëris, all-powerful,
the Sun-god, and autocrat of the nations!

The cangia of Tahoser soon reached the opposite
shore. The boat conveying her *plaustrum** arrived
at the same time, and the oxen which had crossed
over on the flying-bridge were soon yoked to it
by the active servants accompanying them. These
white oxen with black spots wore a kind of tiara,
partly covering the yoke attached to the pole and
secured by two straps, one of which was brought
around the neck, while the other was used as a girth.

Their high withers, large dewlaps, clean-made
and nervous flanks, their pretty hoofs, bright as
agate, and their tails with the tufts carefully
combed, showed that they were of a pure strain and
that the painful labor of the fields had never marred
them. They had the placid majesty of Apis, the
sacred bull, when in the act of receiving offerings and
homage. The exceedingly light plaustrum could
hold two or three persons standing; its semicircular
framework, covered with ornaments and gilding
distributed in gracefully-curved lines, rested upon a
sort of diagonal prop passing above the top, which
the rider took hold of when the way was rough or
the animals were moving at a rapid pace. Revolv-

---

* *Plaustrum*, a travelling-car.— *Wilkinson.*

7*

ing on the axle-tree, set at the back of the framework to prevent jolting, were two wheels with six
spokes, fitted to the axle-ends by small linchpins;
attached to a rod set in the floor of the car was an
open umbrella representing the leaves of the palm.

Nofré, leaning over the front of the plaustrum,
held the reins of the oxen, harnessed like horses,
and drove the car after the Egyptian manner, while
Tahoser, motionless at her side, leaned her hand,
sparkling with rings from the little finger to the
thumb, upon the gilded rim of the shell.

These two beautiful women, one blazing with
jewels and enamels, the other draped in a tunic
of transparent stuff, made a charming group in
the brilliantly-decorated car.   Eight or ten servants,
wearing short drawers with diagonal stripes, pleated
very full in front, accompanied the equipage, accommodating their pace to that of the oxen.

On this side of the stream also the tide of people
was just as great: the inhabitants of the quarter of
the Memnonia and the surrounding villages were
coming in from that direction, and at every moment
the boats discharged their freight upon the brick
quays, bringing new lookers-on to increase the crowd.
Innumerable chariots were on their way towards the
parade-ground, their wheels shining like suns in the
midst of the yellow dust they raised.

Thebes was as empty at this moment as if some
conqueror had carried off its people into captivity.

The frame suited the picture.   In the midst of

luxuriant vegetation, from which the *dôms* were springing like aigrettes, country-houses, palaces, and summer-houses were visible, resplendent with color and surrounded by sycamores and mimosas. Tanks mirrored the sun upon their surfaces, and vines interlaced their tendrils over arched bowers; in the background the gigantic silhouette of the palace of Rameses-Miamun stood out in relief, with its enormous pylons, tremendous walls, and its gilded and painted poles, from which banners were fluttering in the breeze; farther north appeared, in a half-bluish light, the colossal statues,—those mountains of granite in a human form, enthroned, in an attitude of eternal impassibility, before the entrance of the Amenophium, hiding a part of the Ramescum, still more distant, and the tomb of the great priest, but leaving in view at one angle the palace of Menephta.

Nearer the Libyan chain, in the Memnonia quarter, inhabited by the kolchytes, the taricheutes, and the parischites, the red smoke of the natron boilers was rising in the blue atmosphere, for the labor of the grave never ceased, and, though life might run riot outside, bandages must be prepared, cartonages moulded, and coffins covered with hieroglyphics, for some lifeless body was lying on the funeral bier, with lions' or jackals' feet, waiting to be arrayed for the last time.

In the horizon, that seemed nearer on account of the transparency of the air, the Libyan mountains threw into prominence against the pure sky their calcareous peaks, and their arid masses mined by sepulchres and catacombs.

Turning towards the other shore, the view was none the less marvelous: the rays of the sun against the smoky background of the Arabian chain had changed to a rose-color the mammoth pile of the Northern palace, that distance scarcely lessened, and whose mountains of granite and forests of gigantic columns towered above the flat roofs of the dwellings.

In front of the palace stretched a vast esplanade, descending to the river by means of two staircases placed at either end; in the centre an avenue of crio-sphinxes, perpendicular to the Nile, led to an enormous pylon, in front of which were two colossal statues, and a pair of obelisks whose flesh-colored points rising above the cornice stood out, in relief against the cloudless azure of the sky.

In the distance, above the surrounding wall, the lateral face of the temple of Amon presented itself; and farther to the right appeared the temples of Khuns and Opht; a gigantic pylon, visible in profile and facing towards the south, and two obelisks sixty cubits in height, marked the commencement of that prodigious avenue of two thousand sphinxes with the body of a lion and the head of a ram, extending from the Northern to the Southern palace; supported upon their pedestals, you could see the enormous haunches of the first row of these monsters, turning their backs to the Nile as they diverged from each other.

Far away appeared indistinctly, in a rosy light,

the lintels where the mystic globe spread its great pinions, the heads of colossi with a placid expression, the corners of immense edifices, needles of granite, terraces rising one above the other, bunches of palm-leaves springing up like tufts of grass between these huge masses of stone; and the Southern palace displaying its colored walls, its flag-masts, its sloping door-ways, its obelisks, and its troops of sphinxes.

Beyond, as far as the eye could reach, Oph unrolled itself to view, with its colleges of the priests, its palaces, its houses, and the faint blue outlines, indicating in the most distant point of the background the summits of its walls and the tops of its gateways.

Tahoser beheld with indifference this scene already familiar to her, and her absent glance expressed no admiration; but, on passing before a house almost hidden in the thick foliage, she cast aside her apathy and seemed to be searching upon the terrace and in the outside gallery for some familiar face.

A handsome young man leaned nonchalantly against one of the columns of the porch, apparently watching the crowd; but his dark eyes, which seemed absorbed in a dream, did not rest upon the car containing Tahoser and Nofré.

And yet the little hand of the daughter of Peta-mounoph clung nervously to the top of the plaustrum. Her cheeks paled under the faint tinge of color that Nofré had laid on, and, as if overcome with a sudden faintness, she inhaled from time to time the perfume of her bouquet of lotus-flowers.

f

CHAPTER III.

In spite of her usual discernment, Nofré had not observed the effect produced upon her mistress by the disdainful stranger: she had not remarked her pallor followed by a deep blush, the brightening of her eyes, nor the clinking of the enamels and beads of her necklaces, disturbed by the palpitation of her bosom; it is true that her attention was completely taken up in guiding the oxen, which had become a difficult matter in the midst of the constantly-increasing crowd hastening to witness the triumphal entrance of Pharaoh.

At last the chariot reached the field of review, an immense enclosure carefully levelled for the purpose of military parades; embankments that must have taxed for many years the arms of thirty nations carried into captivity framed the gigantic parallelogram; walls of crude brick, forming a talus, were built upon the embankments, and their summits were packed several rows deep with myriads of Egyptians, whose white costumes relieved with bright colors flitted to and fro in the sunlight with the perpetual stir characteristic of multitudes even when they seem to be stationary; back of this cordon of spectators the chariots, curricles, and palanquins, guarded by drivers, bearers, and slaves, made it look like the encampment of a migrating nation; for Thebes, the marvel of the Old World, numbered a greater population than some kingdoms.

The fine and evenly-strewn sand of the vast arena, bordered by a million heads, gleamed from every point under the light that fell from a sky blue as the enamel of the statuettes of Osiris.

On the southern side of the field the wall ended, leaving an entrance from the road going towards Upper Ethiopia, along the Libyan chain. At the opposite angle another break in the talus permitted the road to continue its way through the thick walls towards the palace of Rameses-Miamun.

The daughter of Petamounoph and Nofré, for whom the servants had cleared the way, took up their station at this angle on the summit of the wall to witness the cortège as it passed below.

A tremendous tumult, muffled, deep, and impressive, like an approaching sea, was audible at a distance and overpowered the buzzing of the crowd : as the roaring of a lion drowns the barking of a troop of jackals. Soon the unmistakable tones of instruments were distinguishable in the midst of the confused rumbling produced by war-chariots and the measured tread of infantry ; a reddish mist, like that raised by the wind of the desert, filled the atmosphere in that direction; and yet the breeze had fallen ; there was not a breath of air, and the most delicate leaves of the palm stood motionless as if they were the sculptured capitals of granite pillars; not a tress was lifted from the moist temples of the women, and the fluted ends of their head-dresses hung limply down their backs. The tempest of dust was raised by the marching army, and floated over them like a tawny cloud. The tumult increased; the whirlwinds of dust parted, and the first ranks of musicians entered the immense arena, to the great satisfaction of the multitude, who, notwithstanding their respect for the Pharaonic presence, were growing impatient under the rays of a sun that would have cracked any other skull than that of an Egyptian.

The advance-guard of musicians halted a few moments; the colleges of priests and deputations of the prominent people of Thebes crossed the parade-ground to meet Pharaoh, and ranged themselves in rows, taking care not to interfere with the course of the procession.

The bands, which by themselves might have formed a small army, were made up of drums, trumpets, tambours, and sistra.

The first platoon passed by, sounding a deafening fanfare of triumph from their short brass trumpets that shone like gold. Each musician carried a second trumpet under the arm, as though the instruments were more apt to grow weary than the man. The dress of the trumpeters consisted of a species of short tunic, fastened at the waist by a girdle, with wide ends falling down in front; a fillet, in which there were two ostrich plumes standing apart from each other, bound their thick locks. The way in which the feathers were thrust in reminded one of antennæ and scarabæi, and gave the wearers an odd resemblance to insects.

The drummers, naked to the waist and wearing only a pleated kilt, beat the onager-skin stretched over the ends of their barrel-shaped instruments, hanging from leathern shoulder-belts, with drumsticks of sycamore wood, to the time indicated by the clapping of the hands of a drum-major, who faced them from time to time.

After the drummers came the performers on the sistra, who shook their instruments with an abrupt, jerking movement, making the metal rings rattle over the four bronze rods to a perfect rhythm.

The players on the tympana had their oblong drums slung from a strap passing around the neck, and beat time with their fists on the parchment covering both ends.

Each musical corps counted no less than two hundred men; but the tempest of sound produced by trumpets, drums, sistra, and tympana, although it would have made the ears bleed within the walls of a palace, was none too formidable or too overpowering beneath the vast dome of the sky, in that immense enclosure, in the midst of a restless crowd, and at the head of an army large enough to weary a nomenclator, that was advancing with the sound of a great body of waters.

Was it too much, on the other hand, for eight hundred musicians to precede a Pharaoh, the beloved of Amon-Ra, represented by colossal statues sixty cubits high, carved out of basalt and granite, whose name was inscribed in cartouches upon imperishable monuments, and whose history was engraved and painted on the walls of the hypostyle chambers and on the sides of the pylons in interminable bas-reliefs and innumerable frescoes?

Was it too much, really, for a king who held a hundred conquered races by the hair of the head, and who ruled nations from his lofty throne with a scourge?—for a living Sun, blinding the eyes with its brilliance?—for a god almost immortal?

Following the bands came the captive barbarians, cutting a strange figure: with the face of an animal, a black skin, and woolly hair, they looked more like monkeys than like men, and were dressed in their native costume,—a skirt about the hips, supported by a single bretelle, and embroidered with designs in various colors.

An ingenious and fantastic cruelty had presided over the chaining of these prisoners. Some had their elbows bound together behind their backs; others had them raised above their heads in the most agonizing position imaginable; one set had the wrists secured in wooden manacles; another were throttled in a pillory, or rope, fastening them together in a string, with a knot at the throat of each victim. It seemed as if they had delighted in arranging them in the most painful positions, and in garroting the poor wretches, who advanced before

their conqueror with an awkward, halting step, their
eyes protruding from their heads and their bodies
contorted with suffering.

Keepers walked beside them, keeping them in
order by lashing them with a whip. Bronzed women
with long elf-locks, carrying their children in tat-
tered bits of stuff knotted over the forehead, followed them, shamefaced and crouching, their lean,
misshapen bodies almost naked ; a degraded troop,
sunken to the lowest depths. Others, young and
beautiful, the skin of a lighter tint, the arms adorned
with great bracelets of ivory, and the ears weighed
down with great metal hoops, were clothed in long
tunics with wide sleeves, finished at the neck with a
band of embroidery, and falling in fine ironed pleat-
ings almost to the ankles, tinkling with rings : poor
girls torn from their kindred, their lovers, perhaps,
they still smiled through their tears, for the power
of beauty is unlimited, novelty gives birth to caprice,
and who could tell but that the royal favor might
select one of the captive barbarians for the careful
seclusion of the gynecæum ? Soldiers accompanied
them, protecting them from contact with the crowd.

The standard-bearers came next, holding aloft the
gilded staves of their ensigns, representing the mystic
baris, the sacred hawk, heads of Hathor decorated
with ostrich plumes, winged ibises, historic cartouches, containing the name of the king, crocodiles,
and other symbols of a warlike or religious character. Attached to these standards were long white

streamers, sprinkled with black dots, that fluttered gracefully in the air with the movement of marching. At sight of the standards announcing the approach of Pharaoh, the deputations of priests and notables stretched out their hands in supplication, or let them drop to the knees with the palms turned upward. Some prostrated themselves, their elbows pressed to their sides and their foreheads in the dust, in attitudes of profound adoration and complete submission; the spectators on all sides were waving palm-branches.

A herald, or crier, holding in his hand a roll covered with hieroglyphics, advanced alone, between the ensign- and incense-bearers, preceding the king's palanquin. He proclaimed with a loud voice, sonorous as a trumpet of brass, the victories of Pharaoh; the results of various battles; the number of captives and war-chariots taken from the enemy; the amount of booty; the measures of gold-dust, the elephant tusks, the ostrich plumes, the stores of sweet-smelling spices, the giraffes, lions, panthers, and other rare animals; he cited the names of the barbarian chiefs slain by the arrows and javelins of his Majesty, Aroëris all-powerful, the beloved of the gods.

At every announcement the people raised a tremendous clamor, and from their high post on the walls threw down in the path of the victor the long green branches of palm they were waving. At last Pharaoh appeared. The priests turned towards him

at stated intervals, extending their *amschirs** after
they had thrown incense upon the burning charcoal
in the little bronze cups, supported by a hand running into a sort of sceptre that ended in the head of
a sacred animal, and walked backwards in a reverent
manner as the fragrant blue smoke ascended under
the nostrils of the conqueror, apparently as indifferent
to all these honors as an image of bronze or basalt.

Twelve oëris, or military chiefs, the head covered
with a light casque surmounted by an ostrich plume,
the body naked to the belt, the loins covered with
short drawers laid in stiff pleats, and their bucklers
hanging from their girdles in front of them, bore the
litter, in the shape of a shield, on which rested the
throne of Pharaoh. This was a chair with lions'
feet and arms in the form of a lion, having a high
back covered with a rolling cushion ornamented on
its surface with interlaced blue and pink flowers; the
feet, arms, and entire framework of the throne were
gilded, bright colors filling the spaces where there
was no gilding.

Each side of the palanquin four bearers of flabella
waved their immense semicircular feather fans on
gilded sticks; two priests supported a large cornu-
copia, richly ornamented, from which fell sprays of
enormous lotus-flowers.

Pharaoh wore upon his head a tall helmet like a
mitre, cut away at the ear and descending low in the

---

* *Amschir*, a species of censer.

8*

back to protect the nape of the neck. The blue ground of the casque was strewn with bright spots resembling the eyes of a bird, and consisting of three circles, red, white, and black; the edge was finished with a scarlet and yellow band, and the symbolic viper twisted its golden coils over the front, and rearing itself thrust out its head over the royal brow; two long fluted ends of purple stuff floated over the shoulders, completing this elegant and majestic head-covering.

A wide gorget, made of seven rows of enamels, precious stones, and gold beads, rested upon the breast of Pharaoh, sparkling brilliantly in the sunlight. As upper vestment he wore a sort of *brassière,* divided into a pattern of rose-colored and black checks, the long ends of which passed around the chest several times, binding it tightly; the sleeves, reaching to the biceps and edged with transversal lines of red, gold, and blue, exposed to view the strong, well-moulded arms,—the left one furnished with a wide metal guard to prevent it from being grazed by the bow-string when Pharaoh discharged the arrows from his triangular bow; the right, adorned with a bracelet made of a serpent in several coils, held a long golden sceptre terminating in a lotus-bud. The rest of the body was enveloped in drapery of the finest cambric, laid in innumerable pleats, fastened at the waist by a girdle incrusted with gold and enamels. Between the brassière and belt the torso was visible, shining like rose granite when it is finely polished. Pointed sandals,

like skates, shod the long narrow feet, placed side by
side like the feet of the gods upon the walls of the
temples.

The smooth, beardless face, with pure and noble
features, that looked as if no human emotion could
ever disturb it, and that showed no trace of the vulgar
blood of life, with its deadly pallor, sealed lips, enormous eyes enlarged by black lines, and eyelids as
motionless as those of the sacred hawk, inspired by
its calm alone a reverential dread.

Those fixed eyes seemed to look into eternity and
the infinite, and to take no interest in surrounding
objects. The satiety of enjoyment, the palling of
desires gratified as soon as expressed, the isolation of
the demi-god who has no peer among mortals, the
disgust of adoration, and the ennui even of triumph,
had congealed forever this countenance, implacably
mild and of a granite-like serenity.

Osiris, judging souls, could not have had a calmer
and more majestic mien.

A great tame lion crouched beside him on the litter,
stretching out its enormous paws like a sphinx, and
blinking its yellow eyes.

A cord secured to the litter connected Pharaoh
with the war-chariots of the vanquished chiefs; he
was dragging them after him like animals in a
leash.

These chiefs with a melancholy and savage look,
their elbows bound together with thongs at an awkward angle, rocked to and fro helplessly at the risk

of upsetting their chariots, that were driven by Egyptians.

Next came the war-chariots of the princes of the royal family, each drawn by a span of horses of a pure breed, nobly and elegantly formed, with slender legs, plenty of nerve in the flanks, their manes clipped like a brush, their nodding heads decked with red plumes, and their head-stalls and bridles ornamented with metal bosses.

The curved pole was supported upon a light yoke, bent like a bow with the ends turned up, resting on small scarlet saddles, surmounted by polished brass balls; a girth and breast-band richly quilted and em-broidered, and rich housings with red or blue stripes, and a fringe of tassels, completed this strong, light, and elegant harness.

The body of the car, painted red and green, and decorated with bronze scales and crescents, like the umbo of the bucklers, was flanked by two great quivers, suspended diagonally and pointing in dif-ferent directions, one of which contained the arrows, the other the javelins. On either side a carved and gilded lion, crouching and grinning fiercely, seemed in the act of roaring and springing upon the enemy.

The young princes wore as head-dress a fillet bind-ing their locks, in which was twisted the royal viper with its distended neck; their costume consisted of a tunic, trimmed about the neck and sleeves with a gorgeous embroidery, and confined at the waist with a leather girdle, closed by a metal clasp covered with hieroglyphics; through the belt was thrust a long poniard with a triangular brass blade, the hilt fluted transversely and ending in a hawk's head.

In the chariot beside the prince was the charioteer who drove him in battle, and the attendant whose duty it was to defend the warrior with his buckler while he was engaged in discharging the arrows or throwing the javelins drawn from the quivers on either side.

After the princes came the cars of the Egyptian cavalry, to the number of twenty thousand, each drawn by two horses and containing three men. They advanced ten abreast, the hubs almost striking each other, and yet never touching, so skilful were the charioteers.

Some lighter cars, destined for the purposes of skirmishing and reconnoitring, took the lead, each containing a single warrior, with the reins fastened around the body so as to leave the hands free in battle; he managed his horses by leaning to the right, to the left, or backward, and it was truly marvellous to see these noble animals, who seemed to be left to themselves, preserving a perfectly steady gait under such imperceptible control.

On one of these chariots the tall and graceful figure of Ahmosis loomed up, his glance wandering over the crowd in search of Tahoser.

The prancing of the almost unmanageable horses, the thunder of the wheels with bronze tires, the metallic clatter of arms, lent to the procession an imposing and formidable air, calculated to inspire terror in the bravest heart. The helmets, plumes, and bucklers, the cuirasses covered with green, red, and yellow scales, the gilded bows, the brass swords, glittered and flashed fiercely under the bright rays of the sun looking down over the Libyan chain like a great Osirian eye, and made one feel that the shock of such an army must sweep away nations as a tempest would toss a bit of straw.

Under these countless wheels the earth rumbled and shook with a hollow sound, as though stirred by some inward convulsion.

Succeeding the chariots were the battalions of infantry, marching in orderly array, their bucklers on the left arm, and their weapon, whatever it might be,—hatchet, lance, bow, mace, or sling,—in the right hand; the heads of these soldiers were covered with casques ornamented with two bunches of horsehair, and their bodies were girded with belts of crocodile-skin. With their impassible air, the perfect mechanism of their movements, the copper tint of their skins, heightened by the recent expedition into Upper Ethiopia, and the dust of the desert upon their garments, they inspired admiration for their discipline and courage. With such soldiers Egypt could conquer the world. The allied troops came next, recognizable by the strange form of their helmets, that resembled truncated mitres, or were surmounted by crescents sharpened to a point. Their broad-bladed swords and pointed hatchets must have dealt incurable wounds.

After them came slaves bearing the booty announced by the herald, on their shoulders or on litters, and soldiers were dragging in leash panthers and leopards crouching upon the ground as if to hide themselves, ostriches flapping their wings, giraffes with their long necks towering above the crowd, and even brown bears, taken, it was said, from the Mountains of the Moon.

Long after the king had entered the palace the procession still continued to advance.

On passing the talus at the point where Tahoser and Nofré were stationed, Pharaoh, whose palanquin, borne upon the shoulders of the oëris, raised him above the crowd to a level with the young girl, let his sombre gaze rest upon her: he had not turned his head, not a muscle of his face had stirred, the whole mask remaining as motionless as the golden mask of a mummy; and yet his eyeballs had darted a glance between the stained lids in the direction of Tahoser, and a spark of desire had kindled in their black disks : the effect was as startling as though the granite eyes of the image of some divinity, by a sudden illumination, had expressed a human emotion. One of his hands was lifted slightly from the arm of the throne, a gesture imperceptible to the people gathered there, but remarked by one of his servants walking beside the palanquin, whose eyes glanced in the direction of the daughter of Petamounoph.

However, night had come all at once, for there is no twilight in Egypt; night, or rather a blue day succeeding a yellow one. Upon an azure of infinite transparence innumerable stars lighted their lamps, whose rays trembled confusedly in the Nile, the waters of which were disturbed by the barks bearing to the opposite shore the population of Thebes; and the last cohorts of the army were still unwinding over the field, like the coils of some monstrous serpent, when the cangia of Tahoser stopped at her palace-gate that opened upon the river.

CHAPTER IV.

PHARAOH had reached his palace, situated at a short distance from the field of review on the left bank of the Nile.

In the bluish transparence of the night the immense edifice appeared even more colossal, and its enormous angles stood out in relief against the violet background of the Libyan hills with a sombre and startling effect.

The idea of absolute power attached itself to these immovable masses, over which eternity seemed to glide like a drop of water over marble.

In front of the palace was a great court, surrounded by thick walls finished at the top with concave mouldings; back of this court rose two high columns with capitals of palm-leaves, marking the entrance to a second enclosure. Beyond these columns loomed up a gigantic pylon, made of two immense blocks, a monumental gate better fitted as an entrance for granite colossi than for men of flesh and blood. Beyond these propylons, and occupying the end of a third court, appeared the palace proper in all its formidable majesty : two pavilions, jutting out boldly like the bastions of a fortress, displayed upon their surfaces relieved intaglios of prodigious dimensions, representing, under the consecrated form, the

E   *g*   9

victorious Pharaoh scourging his enemies and tread-
ing them under foot,—unlimited historic pages, inscribed with a chisel in books of stone, for the most
remote posterity to read.

These pavilions ascended much higher than the
pylon, and their cornices, indented and crenellated
with merlons, stood out proudly over the crests of
the Libyan chain in the extreme background of
the picture. Uniting one to the other, the façade
of the palace took up all of the intermediate space.
Above the immense door-way, flanked by sphinxes,
the three tiers of square windows were all aglow,
making the interior illumination visible outside, and
casting a luminous checker-work upon the sombre
wall.

A balcony projected from the first story, supported by figures of captives crouching down upon
a slab.

The officers of the household, the eunuchs, servants, and slaves, notified of the approach of his
majesty by the fanfare of trumpets and rolling of
drums, had come out to meet him, and were waiting,
kneeling or lying prostrate upon the floor of the
court; captives of the miserable race of Schéto,
holding urns filled with salt and olive oil, in which
were floating wicks that burned with a bright clear
flame, stood in a line from the door of the palace to
the first enclosure, as motionless as bronze torch-
bearers.

Soon the first ranks of the procession entered the

palace, and the echoes of trumpets and drums made
such a tremendous noise that the awakened ibises
flew away from the entablatures.

The oëris halted before the door-way of the façade
between the end buildings. Slaves brought steps
and placed them beside the litter; Pharaoh rose
slowly and majestically, and remained standing some
seconds perfectly motionless. Mounted thus upon
a pedestal of shoulders, he towered above their heads
as if he were twelve cubits high, in the strange light
produced by the commingling of the rays of the
rising moon with those of the lamps, and in that
costume, glistening with gold and enamels, he resembled Osiris, or rather a Typhon. He descended
the steps like a statue, and at last entered his palace.

Through a crowd of prostrate slaves and retainers,
Pharaoh crossed over the first inner court, that was
set in a frame of enormous pillars sprinkled with
hieroglyphics and sustaining a frieze ending in a
scroll.

Another court succeeded this, surrounded by a
covered promenade and short, thick columns, upon
whose cone-shaped capitals of hard sandstone rested
a massive architrave.

There was a character of indestructibility about
the straight lines and geometrical forms of this architecture built with quarters of mountains; the pillars
and columns looked as if they were putting forth all
their strength to sustain the weight of the immense
stones resting upon the cubes of their capitals; the

walls, as if they were spreading out in a talus to en-
large their foundations; and the layers, as if they
were welding themselves into a single block; but the
polychrome decorations of the incised bas-reliefs,
enhanced by the great vividness of the solid colors
in the daytime, gave a lightness and brilliance to
these enormous masses, which at night again assumed
their heavy character.

Upon the cornice in Egyptian style, whose rigid
line marked out against the sky a vast parallelogram
of deepest azure, lamps, placed at certain intervals,
flickered in the fitful breeze, the pond in the centre
of the court mingling their red rays with the blue
beams of the moonlight upon its surface; while
rows of small shrubs planted around the basin sent
out a faint sweet perfume.

At the other end stood a door-way leading to the
gynecæum and the private apartments, which were
magnificently decorated.

Beneath the ceiling was a frieze of urœi-serpents,
standing upon their tails and puffing out their
throats. On the entablature of the door-way, in the
bend of the cornice, the mystic globe spread its immense imbricated wings; columns arranged in symmetrical lines supported thick panel-frames of sandstone forming soffits whose blue background was
studded with gold stars. On the walls great carved
pictures, relieved intaglios, colored in the most gorgeous manner, represented the doings of the occupants of the gynecæum, and subjects from private

life. Here Pharaoh was to be seen, seated on his
throne, playing a game of draughts with one of his
wives, standing before him with nothing on but a
fillet binding her locks, in which were thrust sprays
of lotus-flowers. In another picture, Pharaoh, without departing in the least from his royal and sacerdotal impassibility, extending his hand caressed the
chin of a young girl, clad in a necklace and bracelet,
who held up a bouquet for him to inhale its perfume.
Again, he was represented smiling and abstracted, as
if he were affecting indifference, in the midst of the
young queens, who were taxing his gravity with all
manner of graceful and amusing pranks. Other
panels displayed musicians, dancers, and women at
the bath, with their attendants rubbing them and
pouring perfumes over them, all possessing that elegance of pose, youthful delicacy of form, and purity
of features that no art has ever surpassed.

Complicated ornamental designs, of a florid character and perfect execution, in which blue, green, red,
white, and yellow were blended, occupied the open
spaces. Cartouches and bands of a monumental
shape contained the titles of Pharaoh and laudatory
inscriptions.

Winding around the enormous columns, decorative
or symbolical figures, crowned with the pshent and
armed with the *crux ansata,* followed each other in
procession, and, with the pupil of the eye brought
around into the profile, they seemed to be gazing
curiously about the room.

9*

Perpendicular lines of hieroglyphics separated these rows of personages.

The lotus-flowers and buds, appearing among the carved green leaves in their natural colors, made the capitals look like baskets of flowers.

Between every two columns an elegant stand of cedar wood, painted and gilded, supported a bronze lamp filled with scented oil, in which were floating cotton wicks that yielded an agreeable light.

At the base of the columns, in tall vases, alternating with the lamps and united by garlands, were sheaves of golden-stemmed field-grasses and balsamic plants.

In the midst of the apartment there was a round table of porphyry, its disk resting upon the figure of a captive entirely hidden by a collection of urns, vases, jars, and pots containing gigantic artificial flowers,—for real flowers would have had a mean appearance in the midst of this immense room, and it was necessary to establish a proportion between nature and this stupendous work of man. The enormous calyxes were diapered in the most brilliant colors,—golden yellow, azure, and purple.

At the end of the room stood the throne, or fauteuil, of Pharaoh; the legs, crossed in an odd manner and secured by bands winding around them, had at the opening of the angles four statuettes of barbarian prisoners,—Africans and Asiatics, it was plain to be seen, by their physiognomies and costumes. These unfortunate wretches, their elbows tied behind their backs, knelt in an uncomfortable position with the body bent forward, holding upon their humiliated heads the cushion, checkered in gold, red, and black, upon which their conqueror sat.

The muzzles of chimerical beasts, from whose jaws a long red tassel was hanging like a tongue, ornamented the cross-pieces of the seat.

On each side of the throne were ranged, for the princes, fauteuils less rich, but still of an extreme elegance and charming caprice, for the Egyptians were quite as skilful in carving cedar, cypress, and sycamore wood, in gilding, painting, and incrusting it with enamels, as in hewing those monstrous blocks of granite from the quarries of Philæ or Syene for the palaces of their Pharaohs and the sanctuaries of their gods.

The king crossed the apartment with a slow and majestic step and without a quiver of the stained eyelids: there was no indication that he heard the exclamations of devotion or saw the prostrate and kneeling human beings whose temples were brushed by the calasiris rolling about his feet like surf. He mounted his throne, placing his feet side by side and laying his hands upon his knees in the stately attitude of the gods.

The young princes, beautiful as women, took their places right and left of their father. The attendants relieved them of their gorgets of enamels, their girdles and swords, pouring essences upon their locks, rubbing their arms with aromatic oils, and putting garlands of flowers about their necks, fresh-perfumed ornaments,—delicious luxuries better suited to fêtes than the heavy elegance of gold and jewels, and which, moreover, harmonized admirably with everything around them.

Beautiful slaves, whose slender, nude bodies were in the graceful transition from childhood to youth, the hips bound with a narrow girdle, a lotus-flower in the head, and a veined alabaster jar in the hand, gathered timidly around Pharaoh, pouring palm-oil upon his shoulders, arms, and torso, that shone like agate. Other servants waved before him large fans of colored ostrich plumes, fastened to handles of ivory or sandal-wood, that, warmed by their little hands, sent out a delightful fragrance; some held up to Pharaoh's nostrils stems of the nymphæa, with the calyxes expanded like amschir cups. All of these services were proffered him with profound devotion and a species of reverential awe, as if tendered to a divine and immortal being who, out of compassion, had descended from higher spheres to mingle with the vile herd of mankind. For the king was the son of the gods, the beloved of Phré, and the protégé of Amon-Ra.

The women of the gynecæum had risen from their prostrate positions and seated themselves on elegant fauteuils, carved, painted, and gilded, with cushions of red leather stuffed with thistle-down, forming a graceful and smiling group of heads that painters would have loved to reproduce.

The garment of some of them consisted of a tunic
of white gauze, with alternate opaque and transparent stripes, the short sleeves setting free a round
and delicate arm adorned with bracelets from wrist
to elbow; others, naked to the waist, wore a skirt of
a delicate shade of lilac, striped with darker bands
of the same color, over which there was a net-work
of little tubes of rose-colored glass, showing between
the meshes the cartouche of Pharaoh traced upon the
material of the dress; others had red skirts with a
net-work of black beads; a few were draped in a
tissue fine as air or clear as glass, falling in pleats
around them, arranged so as to reveal the pure outline of the bust; some were imprisoned in a scabbard
covered with red, green, and blue scales, clinging
to them like a mould; and others again wore over
the shoulders a pleated cape fastened at the waist by
a sash with flowing ends, and their long skirts were
trimmed with fringe.

There was also much variety in the styles of
coiffure. With some the braided hair ended in
curls; with others it was divided into three parts,—
one falling down the back, the others hanging either
side of the face; and many wore voluminous wigs
with small tight curls and innumerable fine braids,
held in place by transversely-arranged gold cords;
rows of enamels or beads rested like casques upon
these charming young heads, that demanded of art
an unnecessary aid to their beauty.

All of these women held in their hands a lotus-

flower,—pink, blue, or white,—inhaling through
their nostrils, quivering with delight, the penetrating
fragrance arising from the large calyxes. A stem
of the same flower, starting from the nape of the
neck, wound gracefully around the head, letting
its bud fall between the eyebrows, lengthened with
antimony.

Standing in front of them, slaves, wearing nothing
but a girdle about the loins, presented them with
necklaces of flowers, in which were twined white
crocuses with yellow hearts, the purple carthamus,
the helichrysum of a golden tint, the trychos with
its red berries, forget-me-nots whose flowers looked
as if they might have been made of blue enamel,
like the statuettes of Isis, and nepenthes, whose
intoxicating odor makes one forget everything, even
their distant home.

Other slaves followed these, bearing in the upturned palm of the right hand cups of silver or
bronze, filled with wine, and offering with the left
a napkin for drying the lips.

These wines were drawn from amphoræ of clay,
glass, or metal, contained in elegant wicker-baskets
on a stand with four legs, made of a light and pli-
able wood ingeniously bent and interlaced.

The baskets contained seven kinds of wine: date,
palm, and grape, white, red, and pale green, new
wine, wines from Greece and Phœnicia, and white
Marcotic wine with a violet bouquet.

Pharaoh took the goblet from the hands of the

cup-bearer standing beside the throne, and moistened
his lips with the refreshing beverage.

Then the harps, lyres, double pipes, and mandoras
sounded an accompaniment to the triumphal song
executed by choristers ranged before the throne,
kneeling upon one knee, with the other raised, and
keeping time by clapping their hands.

The feast began. The dishes, brought by Ethiopians from the immense kitchens of the palace,
where thousands of slaves were preparing the repast in a blazing atmosphere, were placed upon
tables at a little distance from the feasters ; dishes
of bronze, aromatic wood, earthenware, and porce-
lain enamelled in bright colors, containing quarters
of beef, haunches of antelope, trussed geese, silurus
from the Nile, *pâtes* drawn out and rolled in long
tubes, cakes of sesamum and honey, amethyst- and
amber-hued grapes, green watermelons with a red
heart, and pomegranates full of rubies.

Garlands of papyrus garnished these courses with
their green leaves, the cups were wreathed with
flowers, and in the centre of the tables, out of the
midst of a pile of small loaves with figures and
hieroglyphics stamped upon their white crusts, rose
a tall vase, over which fell sprays from the enormous bunch it contained of persolutas, myrtle, pome-
granate-flowers, convolvuli, chrysanthemums, helio-
tropes, seriphiums, and periplocas, that spread like
an umbel, blending all sorts of colors and perfumes.

Around the socle of the tables, even, were ranged

pots of the lotus. Flowers, flowers,—flowers here, flowers there, flowers everywhere!

They were even placed upon the chairs of the guests; the women wore them around their necks, on their heads, on their arms, as necklaces, garlands, and bracelets; the lamps burned in the midst of immense bouquets, the dishes were hidden among the green leaves, and the wines sparkled in a nest of violets and roses: it was a grand revelry of flowers, a stupendous orgy of aromas of a peculiar character, unknown to other races.

At every moment the slaves brought from the gardens, which they rifled without impoverishing them, armfuls of clematis, rose-laurel, pomegranate-blossoms, xeranthemums, and the lotus, to renew the flowers already faded, while the servants threw nard and cinnamon buds on the charcoal of the amschirs.

When the dishes and the boats in the shape of birds, fish, and chimeras, containing sauces and condiments, had been removed, as well as the ivory, bronze, and wooden spatulas, and the knives of bronze and flint, the guests washed their hands, and the goblets of wine and beer continued to circulate.

The cup-bearer drew with a metal ladle dark and light wines from two large jars of gold, ornamented with figures of horses and rams, that stood on tripods before Pharaoh.

Musicians then appeared, for the chorus had retired: wide tunics of gauze draped their young and graceful forms, veiling them as pure water in a

bath veils the form of the bather; a garland of
papyrus confined their thick locks, touching the
ground with its slender tendrils; a lotus-flower
bloomed upon their foreheads; immense golden hoops
shone in their ears; a necklace of enamels and beads
encircled their throats, and bracelets rattled against
each other on their wrists. One played the harp,
another the mandora, a third the double pipes, managed in a peculiar manner by the hands crossed
over each other, the right upon the left reed, and the
left upon the right; a fourth held a five-stringed
lyre in a horizontal position against the breast; and
a fifth beat the onager-skin stretched over a square
drum. A little girl, seven or eight years old, wearing a belt about the loins and a wreath of flowers on
her head, beat time by clapping her hands.

Dancers entered next: they were slender, willowy,
and lithe as serpents; their great eyes sparkled between the black edges of the lids; long ringlets beat
against their cheeks; some wore ample tunics striped
with blue and white, floating around them like a
cloud; others had on only a simple pleated skirt
reaching to the knees, that gave one a chance to admire the elegant form of the leg and thigh, so full
of strength and nerve.

At first they moved with a slow, gliding step, full
of an indolent grace; then, flourishing the budding
palm-branches, rattling the cylindrical maces ornamented with a head of Hathor, beating the dara-
booka drums with their fists, and running their

thumbs over the parchment of the tambourines, they quickened their steps, bending to and fro, pirouetting, executing *jetés-battus*, and whirling about with a constantly-increasing ardor. But Pharaoh, indifferent and abstracted, did not deign to show the least sign of approval; his fixed eyes were not even looking at them.

They retired blushing and embarrassed, pressing their hands against their beating hearts.

Humpbacked dwarfs with misshapen bodies and club-feet, whose grimaces had the privilege of relaxing the granite-like dignity of Pharaoh, were also unsuccessful: their contortions brought no smile to lips that would not unbend.

To the sound of strange music, produced by triangular harps, sistra, maces, cymbals, and clarionets, Egyptian jesters, wearing tall white mitres of a ridiculous shape, advanced, with three fingers open and two closed, going through grotesque gestures with automatic precision and singing fantastic songs full of discords. His majesty did not even frown.

Women wearing a close cap from which hung three long cords ending in a tassel, their arms and wrists encircled by black leather bands, and wearing short tights fastened by a bretelle passing over the shoulder, went through feats displaying strength and dexterity, each one more surprising than the last, bending themselves, throwing somersaults, tying their dislocated bodies into knots as if they were willow branches, touching the ground with their heads without lifting their feet, and bearing the weight of their companions while in this position.

Others performed feats with one, two, and three balls in succession, throwing them forward, behind the back, with the arms crossed, again seated on the back of one of the women of the troop, or standing on her hip; one even, the most skilful, put a bandage over the eyes like Tmei, the goddess of Justice, so that she could not see, and never missed one of the balls. Pharaoh was insensible to these marvels. He took no interest in the skill of two combatants who, with a wooden guard on the left arm, went through · the exercise of single-stick. The men who threw knives into a block of wood, reaching the centre aimed at with unerring precision, did not amuse him any more than the others. He even put aside the checker-board that the fair Twéa, one of his favorites, presented, offering herself as his opponent; Amensi, Taïa, and Hont-Reché essayed in vain a few timid caresses: he rose and went to his apartments without uttering a word.

The servant who, during the triumphal entry, had noticed the scarcely-perceptible gesture of his majesty, stood at the threshold like a statue. "O king, beloved of the gods," said he, "I left the ranks and crossed the Nile in a punt of papyrus, following the barge of the woman upon whom your hawk-like glance has deigned to fall: she is called Tahoser, and is the daughter of the priest Petamounoph."

Pharaoh smiled, and said, "You have done well!

I will give you a chariot and horses, a pectoral of lapis-lazuli and cornelian beads, and a circle of gold of the weight of green basalt."

In the mean time the deserted women tore the flowers from their hair, rent their gauze robes, and, lying prone upon the polished marble floor, that reflected their beautiful forms like a mirror, wept, crying out, "Ah, one of those accursed barbarian captives has stolen away the heart of our lord!"

CHAPTER V.

On the left bank of the Nile lay the villa of Poëri, the young man who had been the cause of Tahoser's agitation when, upon going to witness the triumphal return of Pharaoh, she had passed in her chariot under the balcony against which the handsome dreamer was nonchalantly leaning.

It was a large estate, partaking of the character of a farm and of a country-seat, occupying, between the shore of the stream and the nearest ridge of the Libyan chain, a vast extent of ground, covered during the season of inundation with a reddish water charged with fertilizing matters, and irrigated during the rest of the year by means of skilfully-contrived canals.

A walled enclosure of limestone, quarried from the neighboring mountains, surrounded the garden, granaries, cellar, and house: these walls, forming a slight talus, were surmounted by acroters with metal points, to prevent any one from climbing them. Three gates, opening in the middle and hinging upon massive imposts ornamented at their capitals with a gigantic lotus-flower, occupied three places in the wall; in lieu of a fourth gate appeared the pavilion, with one of its façades overlooking the garden and the other the road.

This building did not resemble in any way the

h 10*

houses of Thebes: the architect who had planned it had tried to give it, in place of the strong foundations, grand monumental lines, and rich materials of the city structures, a light elegance, a delightful simplicity, and rural grace in keeping with the verdure and repose of the country.

The foundations, which the Nile reached at high water, were of sandstone; the rest was of sycamore wood. Long fluted columns, very slender, like the flag-poles in front of the king's palace, shot up from the ground to the palm-leaf cornice, unfolding the lotus-bud beneath the small cubes of their capitals.

The single story above the ground-floor did not reach the moulding that bordered the terraced roof, thus leaving an open story between its ceiling and the horizontal top of the villa. Short columns with flowering capitals, separated by a long column between each group of four, formed a gallery around this species of apartment hanging in mid-air and swept by every breeze.

Windows, wider at the bottom than at the top of the casement, according to Egyptian rules, and closing with two valves, admitted light to the upper story. The ground-floor was lighted by narrow windows set nearer together.

Above the door-way, finished with two projecting mouldings, depending from the broken lower portion of a parallelogram, was a cross rising from a heart: it was a lucky sentence placed there as a favorable omen,—meaning, as every one knows, "the good abode."

The whole building was painted in soft and pleasing colors, the green capsules of the lotus at the capitals containing sometimes a blue and sometimes a pink flower; the gilded palms of the cornice stood out in relief upon an azure ground; the white walls of the façades were in strong contrast with the painted framework of the windows; and fine lines of red and emerald-green marked out the panels, or interlined the foundation-stones. Outside of the wall of enclosure, that was on a level with the pavilion, stood a row of trees trimmed to a point and forming a screen to ward off the sandy winds from the south that carried with them the heat of the desert. Before the pavilion an immense growth of vines spread their green branches; columns of stone, with the lotus capital placed at symmetrical distances, formed avenues cutting each other at right angles in the vineyard: the branches threw their garlands of green leaves from one to the other, making successive arches of foliage under which one could walk without bending the head.

The earth carefully raked and raised in little ridges about the roots of each vine, relieved with its brown color the bright green of the leaves, among which the birds and sunbeams were flitting to and fro.

Floating on the clear surfaces of two oblong tanks were flowers and aquatic birds. At the angles of these basins four tall palms spread the green nimbus of their foliage like an umbrella over each scaly trunk. The garden around the vineyard was regularly laid out in sections, appropriated to different cultures and separated by narrow paths. In a sort of avenue, that made the circuit of the enclosure, dôm-palms alternated with sycamore-trees; there were square compartments planted with figs, peaches, almonds, olives, pomegranates, and other fruit-trees; some divisions contained nothing but ornamental trees and shrubs, tamarisks, acacias, myrtles, mimosas, cassias, and still rarer varieties found beyond the cataracts of the Nile, under the tropic of Cancer, in the oases of the Libyan desert, and along the borders of the Erythrian gulf; for the Egyptians were much given to the culture of flowers and shrubs, and exacted rare sorts as a tribute from conquered nations.

Flowers of all kinds, varieties of the watermelon, lupine, and onion, were set out in beds; and two ponds of a larger size, supplied by a covered canal leading from the Nile, had small boats on them, ready for the master of the house when he wished to indulge in the pleasures of angling, for fish of every shape and color were darting about in the pure water between the stems and great leaves of the lotus. Masses of luxuriant vegetation surrounded these ponds and trailed over the green surfaces. Beside each basin rose a kiosk with a light roof supported by slender columns and surrounded by a railing, where one could enjoy a view of the waters and breathe the cool morning and evening air reclining upon rustic seats of wood and rushes. This garden, illuminated by the rising sun, had an air of gayety, peace, and happiness. The green of the trees was so vivid, the tints of the flowers were so gorgeous, the air and light bathed the vast grounds so deliciously with their breezes and beams, and the contrast between this rich verdure and the bleached ribs and chalky barrenness of the Libyan chain, rising above the walls and rending the blue sky with its turrets, was so striking, that one felt a longing to halt there and pitch his tent. It was a nest in every way fitted for a dream of happiness.

In the avenues servants were moving about, bearing upon the shoulders a wooden yoke, with clay jars suspended from either end by cords ; these were filled from the reservoirs, and the contents poured into a little hill of earth hollowed out at the foot of each plant. Others were occupied with the *shadoôf* (a bucket hung from a rod revolving upon a stake), supplying a wooden trough that carried water to the driest part of the garden. Pruners were giving the trees a round or elliptical form ; and with the aid of a hoe, made of a wooden blade inserted in a wooden handle and bound to it by a twisted rope, other laborers were bending over, preparing the soil for planting.

It was an agreeable spectacle to see these men, with their crisp black hair and brick-colored bodies, clad in short white drawers, going and coming swiftly and with perfect precision among the bushes, accommodating their steps to the rhythm of a rustic melody. The birds perched upon the trees seemed to know them, and hardly flew away if they chanced to strike a branch in passing.

The door of the pavilion opened now and Poëri appeared upon the threshold. Although he wore the Egyptian costume, his features were not of the national type, and it did not require a second glance to determine that he did not belong to the aboriginal races of the valley of the Nile. And he certainly was not a *Rot-ñ-no.** His delicate aquiline nose, his flat cheek-bones, his serious and firmly-cut mouth, the perfect oval of his face, differed essentially from the African nose, prominent cheeks, full lips, and broad face usual among the Egyptians. The coloring, too, was not the same: the copper-red hue was replaced by a clear olive, slightly tinged with the blush of a pure rich blood; the eyes, instead of rolling between lines of antimony a jet orb, were of a blue dark as the skies at night; the hair, of a softer and more silky texture, did not curl in such rebellious waves; the shoulders did not display that rigid transversal line, repeated as a characteristic feature of the race in the statues of the temples and the frescoes of the tombs.

All of these peculiarities resulted in a rare beauty, which the daughter of Petamounoph could not resist.

---

* The Rot-ñ-no, supposed by M. Champollion to have been the Lydians. — *Wilkinson.*

Since the day when, by chance, Poëri appeared before her, leaning against the balcony of the pavilion, —his favorite post when the occupations of the farm did not demand his presence,—she had often returned there under the pretext of taking a drive, passing in her chariot under the balcony of this villa.

But although she donned her finest tunic, clasped about her neck and wrists her most costly chains and exquisitely-carved bracelets, twined in her locks the freshest lotus-flowers, drew the line of antimony even to her temples, and touched her cheeks with carmine, Poëri did not seem to see her.

And yet Tahoser was very beautiful, and the love which the master of the villa either disdained or ignored, Pharaoh would have paid a high price for: to secure the daughter of the priest he would have given Twéa, Taïa, Amensè, Hont-Réchè, his Asiatic captives, his jars of gold and silver, his gorgets of colored stones, his war-chariots, his invincible army, —all, even his tomb, that, since the commencement of his reign, thousands of workmen had been toiling at down in the darkness.

Love in warm regions, fanned by scorching winds, is not the same thing that it is in hyperborean latitudes, where a calm descends with the hoar-frosts; it is not blood, but fire, that courses in the veins : therefore Tahoser was languishing and pining, in spite of the perfumes she inhaled, the flowers that surrounded her, and the potions she drank to cause oblivion. Music tortured her, or acted too strongly upon her sensibilities; she no longer derived any pleasure from the dances of her companions; at night slumber forsook her eyelids, and, breathless, suffocated, her bosom heaving with sighs, she left her sumptuous couch and stretched herself upon the immense paving-stones of the floor, lying upon her face on the hard granite, as if to allay the fever that consumed her.

The night following the triumphal entry of Pharaoh, Tahoser felt so unhappy, so tired of such an existence, that she determined not to die without having at least made a final effort.

She dressed herself in a garment of common material, wrapped some striped stuff about her head, and took off all her bracelets but one of scented wood; then, when the last rays of light had disappeared, without Nofré, who was dreaming of the handsome Ahmosis, hearing her, she left her room, passed through the garden, drew the bolts of the gate leading to the river, and, walking down to the quay, awakened a boatman, sleeping in the bottom of his canoe of papyrus, who carried her over to the opposite shore.

With tottering steps, and her little hand pressed to her heart to still its beating, she went onward in the direction of Poëri's villa.

It was daylight now, and the gates opened to let the carts and oxen pass out on their way to the labor of the fields, and the herds to the pastures.

Tahoser, kneeling at the threshold, raised her hand

above her head with a supplicating gesture; she was more beautiful than ever, perhaps, in this humble attitude and miserable garb.

Her bosom heaved, and tears streamed down her cheeks.

Poëri saw her, and took her for what she was in fact, a very unhappy woman.

" Enter," said he, " without fear : it is a hospitable dwelling."

CHAPTER VI.

Tahoser, encouraged by Poëri's friendly speech, rose from her supplicating posture. A bright blush suffused her cheeks, but a moment ago so wan: modesty came back with hope; she reddened at the strange act to which love had driven her, and hesitated upon this door-sill that she had so often crossed in imagination, her maidenly scruples, silenced by passion, returning in the presence of reality.

The young man, thinking that timidity, which generally accompanies misfortune, alone prevented Tahoser from entering the house, said to her, in a low, musical voice, penetrated by a slight foreign accent,—

"Enter, young woman, and do not tremble so. The house is large enough to shelter you. If you are weary, you can rest here; if you are thirsty, my servants will bring you fresh water from the porous earthen jars in which it is standing now to cool; if you are hungry, they will give you wheat bread, dates, and dried figs."

The daughter of Petamounoph, encouraged by these hospitable words, entered the house, that justified the inscription of welcome, in hieroglyphics, over its door-way.

Poëri led her into an apartment on the ground-

floor, whose white-coated walls, divided into panels
by the green stems of the lotus ending in a flower,
were very pleasing to the eye. A fine rush matting,
exhibiting designs in various colors, covered the floor;
in each corner of the room, tall vases, standing on
pedestals, were filled to overflowing with immense
bunches of flowers, that shed their fragrance through
the cool shadows of the room.

In the background, upon a low divan, the wood
of which was sculptured into foliage and grotesque
monsters, lay an immense cushion, very inviting to
the weary or luxuriant.

Two chairs, with seats made of Nile rushes inter-
woven, and curved backs supported from without by
perpendicular bars; a set of wooden steps, hollowed
out like a conch, and resting upon three legs; an
oblong table, also on three legs, the border incrusted
with enamels, the urœus-serpent in the centre amid
garlands and agricultural emblems, and a vase standing upon it filled with pink and blue lotus-flowers,
completed a set of furniture that was full of simplicity and rustic grace.

Poëri sat down upon the divan, and Tahoser knelt
in the Egyptian posture before the young man, who
fixed upon her a kindly questioning glance.

She was very lovely in this attitude: the gauze
veil that enveloped her head, falling back, exposed
to view the luxuriant locks, bound with a white
fillet, and the gentle face, so sad and charming.

Her sleeveless tunic left the elegantly-shaped arms

naked to the shoulder, allowing them perfect freedom
of action.

"They call me Poëri," said the young man, "and
I am the steward of the possessions of the crown,
which gives me the right to wear the head-dress
with gilded ram's horns on state occasions."

"My name is Hora," returned Tahoser, who had
arranged her little romance beforehand. "My parents
are dead, and after the sale of their property by the
creditors, only enough remained to meet the funeral
expenses. I am therefore alone and without means;
but, as you have received me under your roof in so
generous a manner, I know how I may be able to
return your kindness. I have been instructed in all
womanly occupations, but my station in life did not
compel me to make use of them. I know how to
spin, to weave linen with different colors running
through it, to embroider flowers and patterns with
a needle on various stuffs; and, moreover, when you
are weary with labor, and the heat of the day enervates you, I can soothe you with a song, the harp,
or the mandora."

"Hora, you are welcome to the house of Poëri.
An occupation shall be found for you suited to a
young girl who has known better days, and that will
not exhaust your strength, for you seem delicate.
There are among my servants some very gentle and
very intelligent young women, who will make agreeable companions for you, and who will show you
how affairs are regulated in this country home. In

the mean time, as one day follows upon another, a better one, perhaps, may dawn for you. If not, you can live on here even to old age in peace and plenty: the guest sent by the gods is sacred."

When he had done speaking, Poëri rose, as if to avoid the thanks of the supposed Hora, who cast herself at his feet, kissing them like some unfortunate being to whom a favor had been granted; but it was love that prompted in this instance, rather than gratitude, and the fresh rosy lips were loath to leave the handsome feet, polished and fair as the jasper feet of the gods.

Before going out to superintend the work upon his lands, Poëri turned on the threshold, and said to Hora,—

"Remain here until a room is prepared for you. I will send you some food by one of my servants."

Then he walked away slowly, the overseer's whip suspended from his wrist. The laborers saluted him by raising one hand to the head and leaning over till the other approached the ground; but it was easy to see from the cordiality of their greeting that he was a kind master. Now and then he stopped to give an order or make a suggestion, for he was well versed in everything pertaining to agriculture and gardening, and then walked on, glancing from right to left and carefully inspecting all that was going on. Tahoser, who had timidly accompanied him to the door and stationed herself upon the threshold, with her elbow on her knee and her chin resting in the palm of her hand, followed him with her glance till he disappeared under the arches of foliage, and still continued to gaze in the direction he had taken long after he had passed through the gate into the fields.

A servant, obeying the order given by Poëri as he passed by, brought upon a tray the thigh of a goose, some onions baked under the ashes, wheat bread, and figs, together with a jar of water, the top of which was covered with myrtle-leaves.

"The master sends you this: eat, young woman, and your strength will return."

Tahoser was not very hungry, but her *rôle* required an appetite: the needy must not slight the offerings of charity. So she ate, and took a long refreshing drink of cold water.

When the servant had gone, she resumed her post of observation. A thousand ideas crowded through her young brain: one moment her maidenly modesty would make her regret the step she had taken; another would find her congratulating herself upon her courage. Again she said to herself, "It is true that I am under Poëri's roof at last; I can see him, if I wish to, every day; I can secretly rejoice in his beauty, more like that of a god than of a man; I can listen to his delightful voice, like music from the soul: but he, who never saw me when I passed under his balcony, dressed in my most brilliant robes, adorned with my costliest jewels, bearing about me the perfumes of essences and flowers, mounted in a gilded and painted chariot, shaded by

an umbrella, and surrounded with a train of attendants like a queen, will he be more apt 'to notice a
poor supplicant, an object of charity and clad in
mean garments?

"Will my misery be able to accomplish what my
wealth could not? Perhaps, after all, I am ugly,
and Nofré was only flattering me when she pretended
that from the undiscovered sources of the Nile to the
point where it empties into the sea there is no more
beautiful woman to be found than her mistress.
But no, I must be beautiful: the admiring eyes of
men have revealed it to me a thousand times, and,
more than that, the spiteful manner and disdainful
expression of the women I meet. Will Poëri, who
has inspired such a mad passion in my heart, ever
love me?

"He would have shown the same kindness to any
old woman with wrinkled brow and sunken chest,
wrapped in hideous rags, and her feet gray with dust.
Any one else but he would have recognized instantly,
under Hora's disguise, Tahoser, the daughter of the
great priest Petamounoph; but he never condescended
to look at me, any more than a god of basalt does at
the devotees that offer up to him quarters of antelope
and bouquets of lotus-flowers."

These reflections cooled the courage of Tahoser;
but she gathered confidence again in repeating to herself that her youth, her comeliness, her love, would
succeed finally in melting this insensible heart: she
would be so gentle, so attentive, so devoted, she would

make her poor toilet with so much art and so much coquetry, that surely Poëri could not resist. Then at last she would make known to him that the humble servant was a lady of rank, owning slaves, estates, and palaces, and in imagination she arranged as a sequel to this obscure felicity a life of happiness, both gay and splendid.

"First of all, I must make myself attractive," said she, rising and going towards one of the ponds.

When she had reached it, she knelt upon the stone margin and bathed her face, neck, and shoulders; the disturbed water showed her, within its mirror shivered into a thousand bits, her own image confused and trembling, smiling at her as if through a green gauze, and the little fish, seeing her shadow and thinking that she was going to throw them some crumbs, came to the edge in shoals.

She gathered two or three lotus-buds, lying upon the surface of the tank, and twined the stems through the fillet binding her hair, arranging a head-dress that Nofré's skill could not have equalled, even if she had emptied all of her jewel-cases.

When she had finished, she rose fresh and radiant, while a tame ibis, who had been gravely watching her operations, stretched himself to his full height, craned out his long neck, and clapped his wings two or three times as if in applause.

Her toilet completed, Tahoser returned and took up her post again at the door of the pavilion, waiting for Poëri.

The sky was of an intense blue; the light trembled in visible waves through the transparent atmosphere; intoxicating perfumes ascended from the plants and flowers; birds flitted about among the palm-branches, pilfering berries; butterflies chased each other, dancing lightly upon the wing.

Human activity bore a part in this joyous scene, and, lending animation to it, made it still more attractive. Gardeners came and went; here and there servants appeared carrying bunches of herbs and vegetables, while others stood under the fig-trees receiving in baskets the fruit thrown to them by trained monkeys perched upon the topmost branches.

Tahoser regarded with ecstasy all of this fresh outdoor life, whose calm penetrated her very soul, and thought within herself,—

"Oh, how happy it would make me to be loved here in the midst of light, perfume, and flowers!"

Poëri reappeared now: his tour of inspection was ended, and he retired to his apartments to escape the scorching hours of day.

Tahoser followed him timidly, standing near the door, ready to depart at the slightest signal; but Poëri motioned her to remain. She advanced a few steps and knelt upon the mat.

"You tell me, Hora, that you know how to play the mandora: take down yonder instrument hanging upon the wall, sound the strings, and sing to me some ancient melody, very sweet and very slow. Slumber is full of enchanting visions when rocked by music."

i

The daughter of the priest took down the mandora, approached the couch on which Poëri was reclining with his head resting upon the wooden pillow in the shape of a crescent, stretched her arm along the neck of the instrument, and, pressing the body against her beating heart, swept her hand over the strings, striking some chords. Then she sang with a very true voice, although it trembled a little, an old Egyptian air, a vague sigh of her forefathers, transmitted from generation to generation, in which a certain phrase returned from time to time, very sweet and penetrating in its monotony.

"Well," said Poëri, turning his dark-blue eyes upon the young girl, "you have not deceived me. You understand rhythm as well as a professional musician, and you might display your art in royal palaces. But you give a new meaning to your song. It seems as if you were composing the air that you sing, and that gives it a magical charm. Your face does not look at all as it did this morning; another woman seems to shine through you, like a light through some transparent stuff. Who are you?"

"I am Hora," responded Tahoser: "have I not already told you my history? Only I have washed the dust of the roads from my face, smoothed the rumpled folds of my dress, and put a flower in my hair. If I am poor, it is no reason why I should be ugly, and the gods sometimes refuse a fair face to the rich. But shall I continue?"

"Yes; repeat the same air: it fascinates and bewilders me, and destroys consciousness like the nepenthes: repeat it until sleep descends with forgetfulness upon my eyelids."

Poëri's eyes, fixed upon Tahoser at first, began shutting gradually until they were entirely closed. The young girl still played on softly, repeating the refrain of her song in an undertone till it died away. Poëri slept; she stopped, and began to fan him with a fan made of palm-leaves, that was lying on the table.

Poëri was handsome, and sleep lent to his pure features an ineffable expression of languor and tenderness; the long lashes resting upon his cheek seemed to hide some celestial vision, and the beautiful crimson lips, half opened, moved as if addressing inaudible words to some invisible being.

After a long contemplation, emboldened by silence and solitude, Tahoser, scarcely knowing what she did, leaned over the brow of the sleeper, and, holding her breath and pressing her hand to her heart, imprinted upon it a frightened, momentary, and furtive kiss; then she rose up, ashamed and blushing deeply.

The sleeper had been vaguely conscious, in his dreams, of Tahoser's kiss; he sighed, and murmured in Hebrew, "O Rachel, my beloved Rachel!"

Fortunately, these words in an unknown tongue were meaningless to the daughter of Petamounoph; and she took up the palm-leaf fan again, hoping and fearing that Poëri would awaken.

CHAPTER VII.

WHEN day had dawned, Nofré, who slept on a little cot at her mistress's feet, was surprised not to hear Tahoser calling to her and clapping her hands, as usual. She raised herself upon her elbow and found that the bed was empty. And yet the first rays of light, falling upon the frieze of the porch, had just commenced to cast the shadows of the capitals and the upper portion of the columns on the wall.

Tahoser was not accustomed to such early rising, and scarcely ever left her couch without having her women there to wait upon her; besides, she had never gone out before without first having her hair arranged after the night's rest, and scented water poured over her, as she sat in the bath with her arms folded over her breast. Nofré, alarmed, threw on a transparent dress, thrust her feet into sandals made of palm-fibres, and went in search of her mistress. She first examined the porches of the two courts, thinking that Tahoser, unable to sleep, might have gone out to inhale the freshness of the dawn in these sheltered walks.

Tahoser was not there.

"I will examine the garden," said Nofré to herself: "perhaps she may have taken it into her head to see how the dew looks sparkling among the leaves of the plants, or to watch the unfolding of the buds."

The garden, thoroughly investigated, was quite deserted. Nofré went through avenues, vineyards, arbors, and groves, to no purpose. She entered the summer-house at the end of the vineyard; no Tahoser was to be found there. She ran to one of the tanks, where her mistress might have taken a fancy to bathe, as she did sometimes, accompanied by her attendants, on the granite staircase that led down to the sand-covered bottom of the basin.

The great leaves of the nymphæa, floating upon the surface, did not seem to have been disturbed; the ducks, plunging their azure throats into the smooth water, were all that ruffled it, and they welcomed Nofré with joyous cries. The faithful maid began to be seriously frightened; she summoned the household; slaves and attendants left their cells, and, informed by Nofré of the strange disappearance of Tahoser, began to make a very careful search; they went up on the terraces, examined every room, and searched every nook or corner where there was a possibility of finding her. Nofré, in her anxiety, even went so far as to open the chests where her robes were kept, and the cases containing her jewels, as if these boxes might have held her mistress.

Tahoser was certainly not in the house.

An old servant, with consummate shrewdness, conceived the idea of inspecting the sand in the

avenues, to try and find the trace of his mistress's
footprints: the heavy bolts of the gate leading to the
town were in their places, and did away with the
supposition that Tahoser might have gone in that
direction. It was true that Nofré had run hither
and thither over all the paths, leaving the marks of
her sandals; but, stooping close to the ground, old
Souhem was not long in discovering, among Nofré's
footprints, the outline of a slim, delicate sole, belonging to a much smaller foot than that of the maid.

He followed this trace, which led him through the
grape-arbors, by the pylon of the court, to the river-
gate. The bolts, as he made Nofré observe, had
been drawn, and the leaves came together only by
means of their weight: so the daughter of Petamounoph must have gone out that way.

The footprints disappeared on the other side. The
brick quay had nothing to show. The boatman who
had taken Tahoser across had not returned to his
station. The others were asleep, and, when interro-
gated, replied that they had not seen anything. One,
however, told them that a woman, poorly clad, had
gone over very early towards the Memnonia quarter, no doubt to attend to some funeral ceremony.
This description, which did not in any manner apply
to the elegant Tahoser, completely upset all of Nofré's
and Souhem's ideas.

They entered the house again, downhearted and
disappointed. The servants and slaves seated themselves on the ground in forlorn attitudes. Letting one

haud hang down with the palm upturned, and laying
the other upon the head, they exclaimed in chorus,
as if singing a dirge, "Alas! alas! alas! our mistress has left us!"

"By Oms, dog of the infernal regions, I will find
her again," said old Souhem, "if I have to go in the
body to the utmost limits of the occidental regions,
the road that the dead travel. She was a good mistress; she gave us an abundance of food, did not
oppress us with work, and had our beatings admin-
istered with justice and moderation. Her foot rested
lightly upon the bowed neck, and under her roof a
slave might fancy himself free."

"Alas! alas! alas!" repeated the men and women,
throwing dust upon their heads.

"Alas! dear mistress, who can tell where you are
now?" cried the faithful attendant, with tears streaming down her cheeks. "Perhaps some magician has
forced you, by means of a powerful charm, to leave
your palace, so that he may weave some dreadful
spell over you: what if he should cut and tear your
beautiful body, pluck out your heart through an
opening in the side like a parischite, and cast the
remains to a crocodile, so that on the day of reunion
your mutilated soul will find nothing but shapeless
pieces? And we cannot lay you beside the painted
and gilded mummy of your father, the great priest
Petamounoph, in the funeral crypt prepared for you
in that tomb of which the kolchyte keeps a plan!"

"Calm yourself, Nofré," said old Souhem; "you

must not give way to despair so quickly; perhaps
Tahoser will soon return. No doubt she has yielded
to some impulse that we know nothing of, and in a
short time we may see her coming back gay and
smiling, her hand full of water-lilies."

The attendant, drying her eyes with one corner of
her robe, signified her compliance. Souhem squatted
down, with his knees bent up like the cynocephalous
images rudely carved from a block of basalt, and,
holding his temples in the dry palms of his hands,
seemed to meditate profoundly. His skin of a reddish brown, his sunken eyes, his prominent jaws, his
deeply-wrinkled cheeks, and the stiff hair standing
out like bristles around his face, completed his resemblance to the gods with simian heads: he certainly
was not a god, however, though he looked wonder-
fully like a monkey. The result of his musing,
anxiously waited for by Nofré, was this:

"The daughter of Petamounoph is in love."

"Who told you so?" cried Nofré, who imagined
that she was the only one who could read her mistress's heart.

"No one; but Tahoser is very beautiful. For sixteen seasons she has witnessed the rise and fall of
the Nile. Sixteen is the age when love begins to
awaken, and of late she has summoned her harp-,
mandora-, and flute-players at unusual hours, like
one who wishes to calm some heart-trouble with
music."

"You reason very well, and you have some wisdom in that old bald pate of yours; but where did you gain your knowledge of women, you who never do anything but hoe the garden and carry water-jars on your shoulders?"

The slave grinned broadly, showing two rows of long white teeth, strong enough to crack date-stones; and this grimace seemed to say, " I have not always been old, and in bondage."

Her suspicions aroused by Souhem's suggestion, Nofré thought at once of the handsome Ahmosis, Pharaoh's oëris, who passed so often under their terrace, and who graced his war-chariot so well in the grand triumphal entry. Now, she loved him herself, without being aware of it, and she charged these feelings to her mistress's account. She put on a thicker robe, and went to the officer's house, perfectly convinced in her own mind that she should find Tahoser there. The young oëris was reclining on a low divan at one end of his room. On the walls were grouped, as trophies, different weapons : the leather corselet covered with bronze scales, engraved with Pharaoh's cartouche; the brass dagger, with its handle of jade, pierced, evidently, for the purpose of letting the fingers pass through; the battle-axe with its blade of flint, the falchion with curved blade, the casque with ostrich plumes, the triangular bow, and arrows with red feathers at the end ; honorary collars lay upon the tables, and some open chests displayed booty taken from the enemy.

When he saw Nofré, whom he knew well, stand-

ing upon his threshold, Ahmosis experienced a keen
sensation of pleasure; his brown cheeks flushed, a
thrill ran through his nerves, and his heart beat fast.

He believed that Nofré had brought him some mes-
sage from Tahoser, although the priest's daughter had
never returned his glances. But a man whom the
gods have endowed with beauty readily believes that
every woman fancies him.

He rose, and took several steps towards Nofré,
whose anxious eyes were peering into every corner of
the room, to make sure of the presence or absence of
Tahoser.

" What brings you here, Nofré ?" asked Ahmosis,
seeing that the young attendant, who was taken up
with her investigation, was not going to break the
silence.

" Your mistress is well, I hope, for I think that
I saw her yesterday, assisting at the entrance of
Pharaoh."

" You should know better than any one else how
my mistress is," replied Nofré, " for she fled from
home without telling any of us her plans, and I
would have sworn by Hathor that you knew her
place of refuge."

" She has disappeared ? What do you mean ?"
cried Ahmosis, with an astonishment that certainly
was not feigned.

" I thought that she loved you," said Nofré, " and
sometimes the most reserved young girls do the wild-
est things. She is not here, then ?"

" The god Phré, who knows everything, knows where she is; but none of his rays armed with hands have found their way into my house. You can look around, if you wish to, and examine my rooms."

" I believe what you tell me, Ahmosis, and I will go away; for, if Tahoser were here, you would not hide it from the faithful Nofré, who would ask nothing better than to serve you both. You are handsome, she is young, rich, and free. The gods would have looked down upon your union with pleasure."

Nofré returned home more disturbed and puzzled than before. She feared that the household might be suspected of having murdered Tahoser for the sake of her wealth, and that they might be beaten to make them confess something that they did not know.

Pharaoh, on his side also, was thinking of Tahoser. After having made the libations and offerings required by the ritual, he seated himself in the inner court of the gynecæum, and fell into a revery, without paying any heed to the pastimes of his women, who, crowned with garlands of flowers, were amusing themselves in the pellucid tank, throwing water over each other, and laughing loudly to attract the attention of their lord, who had not decided yet as to who should be the queen of the week.

They made a charming tableau, these beautiful women, with their slender figures, like submerged statues of jasper, in that frame of shrubs and flowers, in the midst of a court surrounded by columns painted in brilliant colors, and under the pure light of a sky of azure, traversed from time to time by an ibis, with its beak buried in its breast and its legs trailing in its wake.

Amensé and Twéa, tired of swimming, had left the water, and were kneeling on the edge of the basin, spreading out their luxuriant masses of hair to dry in the sun, the ebon locks making their skin look still fairer; the last crystal drops were rolling off from their lustrous shoulders and arms polished like jade; servants were rubbing them with essences and aromatic oils, and a young Ethiopian girl waved before their nostrils an immense flower.

It seemed as if the artists who sculptured the bas-reliefs decorating the halls of the gynecæum had taken these graceful groups as models; but Pharaoh could not have looked with a colder eye upon the stone carvings.

Mounted upon the back of the fauteuil was a tame monkey, chattering and munching dates; and a pet cat was rounding its back and rubbing itself against its master's legs; when all at once a mis-shapen dwarf pulled the monkey's tail and the cat's whiskers, making one scold and the other spit. This generally provoked a smile from his majesty; but his majesty was not inclined to laugh to-day. He drove away the cat, made the monkey get down from the chair, struck the dwarf on the head with his fist, and strode away to his apartments of granite. Each one of these rooms was built of blocks of an immense size, and closed by stone doors that no human power could have forced without knowing how they were made to open.

In these rooms Pharaoh kept his treasures and the booty taken from conquered nations. There were ingots of precious metals ; crowns of gold and silver ; breastplates and bracelets of cloisonné enamels ; earrings that shone like the disk of Moui ; collars with sextuple rows of cornelian, lapis-lazuli, blood-stone, pearls, agates, sardonyx, and onyx ; anklets of beautiful workmanship ; belts with golden scales engraved with hieroglyphics ; rings with scarabæi at the collets ; strings of fish, crocodiles, and hearts in stamped gold ; serpents of enamel in several coils ; vases of bronze ; jars of veined alabaster and blue glass, over which white spirals were winding ; caskets of enamelled ware ; boxes of sandal-wood in strange and fantastic shapes ; heaps of gums and spices from all lands ; ebony blocks ; costly stuffs, fine enough to draw through a ring ; black, white, or colored ostrich plumes ; elephants' tusks of a prodigious size ; goblets of gold, silver, and gilded glass ; and small statuettes of excellent material and workmanship.

In each room Pharaoh made two stout slaves, of the Kousch and Schéto races, take what they could carry on a litter ; then, striking his hands together, he called Timopht, the servant who had sought out Tahoser, and said to him,—

"Have this taken to Tahoser, the daughter of Petamounoph, as a gift from Pharaoh."

Timopht took the head of the cortège, and before long the slaves arrived with their burden at Tahoser's house.

"For Tahoser, on the part of Pharaoh," announced Timopht, knocking at the door.

At sight of these treasures Nofré nearly fainted, half from fear and half from amazement: she was afraid that the king would kill her when he learned that the daughter of the priest was missing.

"Tahoser has gone away," said she, in answer to Timopht, "and I swear by the four sacred geese, Amset, Sis, Soumauts, and Kebh-senu, flying at the four quarters of the wind, that I do not know where she is."

"Pharaoh, the favorite of Phré, the beloved of Amon-Ra, has sent these presents. I dare not return them. Keep them until she appears again. You will have to answer for them with your head. Have them locked up in some room and watched by reliable servants," replied the messenger from the king.

When Timopht returned to the palace, and, prostrate with his elbows pressed against his sides and his forehead in the dust, announced that Tahoser had disappeared, the king flew into a passion, and struck the floor such a blow with his sceptre that he cracked one of the stones.

CHAPTER .VIII.

Tahoser, it must be confessed, had scarcely bestowed a thought upon Nofré, her favorite maid, or the anxiety that her absence would cause.

This dear mistress had quite forgotten her grand house at Thebes, her servants, and all her finery,—a strange and incredible thing for a woman.

The daughter of Petamounoph knew nothing of Pharaoh's love for her: she had not observed the look full of longing that found its way down to her from the lofty pinnacle of all that majesty that nothing on earth could move; if she had seen it she would have laid the royal favor, as an offering among all the flowers of her soul, at Poëri's feet.

While pushing the spindle with her toe to make it ascend the length of the thread, for this was the task that had been assigned her, she followed every movement of the young Hebrew out of the corner of her eye, her glance resting upon him like a caress: she silently enjoyed the happiness of being near him in the pavilion to which he allowed her access.

If Poëri had turned his head towards her he would no doubt have been struck with the humid light in her eyes, the sudden blush that would pass over her lovely cheeks like a rose-colored cloud, and the quick pulsations of her heart, betrayed by the fluttering of her bosom. But, seated at a table, he was bending over a sheet of papyrus, dipping a reed into the cavity, containing ink, in an alabaster tablet, and casting up his accounts in demotic characters.

Was Poëri conscious of Tahoser's plainly-visible love for him? Or had he some private reason for appearing to ignore the fact? His conduct towards her was gentle and kindly, but reserved, as if he wanted to avoid or prevent some unwelcome confession which it would have pained him to answer. And yet the assumed Hora was very beautiful; her charms were only enhanced by the meanness of her dress, and, just as one sees, in the warmest part of the day, a luminous vapor in motion above the glistening earth, so an atmosphere of love seemed trembling around her. On her parted lips her secret hovered like a bird about to take wing; and low, very low, when she was sure of not being heard, she would murmur to herself, like an ever-recurring theme, "Poëri, I love you."

It was harvest-time, and Poëri went out to oversee the laborers. Tahoser, who could not tear herself away from him, any more than the shadow can separate itself from the body, followed him timidly, fearing that he might order her to remain at the house; but the young man said to her, in a voice that had no accent of displeasure in it,—

"A sight of the peaceful employments of agriculture often brings rest to the troubled soul, and if any mournful recollection of departed happiness oppresses

.you, it will vanish in the presence of such cheerful activity. These things must be new to you; for your skin that has never been exposed to the sun, your delicate feet and hands, and the elegance with which you drape the coarse stuff that serves you as a garment, all prove to me that you have always lived in the city, in the midst of luxury and refinement. Come, sit down and turn your spindle under the shade of this tree, where the harvesters have hung up their leather bottles to cool."

Tahoser obeyed, and sat down under the tree, with her arms folded upon her knees and her knees even with her chin.

The plain extended from the wall of the garden to the first slopes of the Libyan chain, like a yellow sea rolling with golden waves under the faintest breeze.

The light was so intense that here and there the golden tone of the wheat blanched to silver. In the rich deposit of the Nile the blades had grown strong, thick, and tall as javelins, and never was there a richer harvest spread out beneath the sun, blazing and crackling with heat; there was enough to fill to overflowing the row of granaries, with vaulted roofs, beside the wine-cellars.

The reapers had been at work for some time, and their shaven or curly heads, covered with a white cloth, and naked, brick-colored bodies, were visible at a distance among the waving grain. They bent forward and rose again with a regular movement, mowing the wheat with their sickles just beneath

the car, with as much precision as if they were following a line marked out by a cord. After them,
in the furrows, came the gleaners, with sacks of matting, in which they gathered the fallen ears, and,
slinging them over their shoulders, or fastening them
to a wooden bar, with the help of a comrade they
carried them to the mill-stones, placed at a little
distance from each other.

Sometimes the tired reapers stopped to breathe,
and, throwing the reaping-hook under the right
arm, took a drink of water, then resumed their
work quickly, fearing the overseer's stick ; the har-
vested ears were spread out on the threshing-floor in
heaps, levelled by a fork, and slightly raised at the
edges by the new bagfuls poured out there.

Poëri then made a sign to the oxherd to bring up
his animals. They were superb creatures, with long
horns spreading out like the head-gear of Isis, high
withers, big dewlaps, and slender legs full of nerve.

The mark of the farm had been stamped upon
their haunches with a hot iron. They marched
along gravely, bowed down under the horizontal
yoke uniting the four heads.

They were led to the threshing-floor, and, urged
on by a whip with a double lash, began to move
around in a circle, making the grain fly out of the
ear with their cloven hoofs. The sun shone upon
their glossy coats, and the dust they raised mounted
to their nostrils ; so that, after twenty rounds, they
leaned against each other and slackened their steps

perceptibly, in spite of the lashes that whistled about their flanks. To spur them on, the driver, who was guiding the animals by hanging to the tail, started, to a quick and lively measure, the old song of the oxen,—

"Turn for yourselves; O oxen, turn for yourselves; measures for yourselves, and measures for your masters!"

And the animals, aroused, moved onward, disappearing in a cloud of light dust sparkling with golden motes.

The work of the oxen done, men appeared, armed with wooden scoops, who threw the wheat upward and let it fall again to separate it from the straw, the beards, and the husks.

The wheat, winnowed in this manner, was put into sacks, noted down by a scribe, and carried up a flight of steps to the granaries.

Tahoser, under the shade of her tree, enjoyed this spectacle full of life and grandeur, and often her absent hand would forget to twist the thread. The day was advancing, and already the sun that rose on the other side of Thebes had crossed the Nile, and was on its way towards the Libyan hills, behind which its disk descended every night. It was the hour when the animals return from the fields and re-enter the stables. Stationed near Poëri, she witnessed this grand pastoral procession.

First came an immense drove of oxen, some white, others red; one lot was black spotted with white, another piebald, while some were marked with dark stripes; they were of every hue and shade. As they passed they raised their lustrous muzzles, from which the foam hung in filaments, and opened their great mild eyes. The most impatient, scenting the stables, rose up so that their heads showed above the crowd of horns a few seconds, then they fell back again, and could not be distinguished from the rest. The less active, left in the rear by their companions, as if protesting against it, bellowed in a prolonged and plaintive manner.

Beside the cattle marched the oxherds, with their whips and coils of rope.

When they came in front of Poëri they knelt, and, with their elbows pressed to their sides, touched the ground with their foreheads in token of respect.

The scribes wrote down the number of heads of cattle upon their tablets.

Asses followed the oxen, trotting along and kicking under the sticks of the shaven-headed drivers, who wore a cloth about the loins with the ends falling down in front; the animals filed along, shaking their immense ears, and hammering the ground with their hard little hoofs.

The ass-drivers made the same genuflection as the oxherds, and the scribes also took down the exact number of their animals.

The goats came next in turn; they advanced headed by the bucks, their thin, cracked voices trembling with delight. The goatherds had some difficulty in curbing their impatience, and bringing back the marauders that strayed away from the body of the army. They were counted like the oxen and asses, and, with the same ceremony, the goatherds prostrated themselves at Poëri's feet.

The last in the procession were the geese, who, tired of walking, waddled along on their great webbed feet, clapping their wings noisily, stretching out their necks and giving vent to a harsh hissing sound. Their number was also marked down, and the tablets handed over to the steward of the place.

Long after the oxen, asses, goats, and geese had gone in, a column of dust, that the wind could not sweep away, mounted slowly upward.

"Well, Hora," said Poëri to Tahoser, "has the spectacle of the harvesting, and of the herds and flocks, amused you? These are the recreations of the country; we have not here, as they have at Thebes, musicians and dancers. But agriculture is a sacred thing: man depends upon it; and he who sows a grain of wheat performs an act pleasing to the gods. Now go and take your supper with your companions; as for me, I am going back to the pavilion, to run over my accounts and see how many bushels the ears have yielded."

Tahoser, lowering one hand to the ground, and placing the other upon her head, in token of her respectful acquiescence, departed.

In the eating-room several young women were chatting, laughing, and eating raw onions, cakes of *doura*, and dates; a little vase filled with oil, in which a wick was floating, illuminated the room, as night had fallen, shedding a yellow light upon their brown cheeks and dusky torsos unshielded by any drapery.

Some were seated on plain wooden stools; others, kneeling upon one knee, leaned their backs against the wall.

"Where can the master be going in this way every night?" said a little girl, maliciously, peeling a pomegranate with the pretty airs of a monkey.

"The master goes where he has a mind to," said a tall slave, chewing the petals of a flower: "must he render to you an account of his doings? You wouldn't be the one, at any rate, to keep him here."

"Why not me as well as any one else?" replied the offended child.

The tall girl only shrugged her shoulders.

"Hora herself, who is whiter and handsomer than any of us, could not do it. Although he bears an Egyptian name, and is in the service of Pharaoh, he belongs to the barbarous race of Israel; and he goes out at night no doubt to assist at the sacrifice of children, which the Hebrews celebrate in desert places, where owls screech, hyenas yell, and serpents hiss."

Tahoser left the room quietly, without saying a word, and crouched down in the garden behind a clump of mimosas. After she had waited two hours she saw Poëri start out into the country.

Then she began to follow him, softly and silently as a shadow.

CHAPTER IX.

Poëri, who was armed with a stout palm-stick, went towards the river, over a narrow causeway running through a field of submerged papyri, that, leafy at the base, sent up on either side their rectilinear stalks, from six to eight feet in height and ending in a tuft of fibres, reminding one of the lances of an army drawn up for battle.

Holding her breath, and gliding along on tiptoe, Tahoser started after him down the narrow road. There was no moon that night, and, if there had been, the dense growth of papyrus would have afforded sufficient protection for the young girl, who kept a little in the rear.

After leaving this it was necessary to cross an open space. The supposed Hora, allowing Poëri to get some distance in advance, crouched down, and, making herself as small as possible, crawled along the ground.

A mimosa grove followed, and, hidden among the thickets, Tahoser could move onward without so much precaution. She was so close to Poëri, whom she was afraid of losing in the darkness, that often the branches that he put aside struck her in the face; but she did not mind it: a feeling of intense jealousy urged her on to solve the mystery which she did not interpret in the same manner as the servants of the house.

She did not for an instant believe that the young Hebrew went out every night to take part in some infamous and barbarous rite: she was sure that a woman must be the cause of these nocturnal excursions, and she longed to know her rival.

The indifferent kindness of Poëri was proof enough that his heart was already occupied: otherwise could he have remained insensible to charms that were celebrated throughout Thebes, as well as all Egypt, or would he have feigned to be unconscious of a love that would have filled with pride any of Pharaoh's officers, the chief priests, basilico-grammats, or even princes of the royal family?

Arrived at the bank of the river, Poëri descended some steps cut in the steep wall, and leaned over as if he were untying a rope. Tahoser, lying flat down on the top of the bank, with her head over the edge, saw to her great chagrin that the mysterious wanderer was undoing a little canoe of papyrus, long and slim as a fish, in which he was preparing to cross the stream. He sprang, in fact, into the boat, pushing it away from the shore with his foot, and moved off, managing the single paddle placed at the back of the frail bark.

The poor girl wrung her hands in despair: she was about to lose the clue to this secret that it was so important for her to know.

What should she do? Retrace her steps with her

heart a prey to doubt and uncertainty, the worst of all evils? She summoned up her courage, and soon determined what to do. To search for another canoe was not to be thought of for a moment.

Letting herself glide down the talus, she pulled off her dress in a trice and wound it about her head; then she slid into the stream, taking care not to make it foam.

Lithe as a water-snake, she moved her beautiful arms about in the dark stream, where the magnified reflections of the stars were trembling, pursuing the boat at a distance.

She swam admirably; for every day she was accustomed to exercise with her women in the vast pond of her palace, and none were so skilful in the art as Tahoser.

The currents, smooth at this spot, did not offer much resistance; but in the middle of the river, so as not to drift with them, she had to use her feet and arms vigorously among the boiling eddies. Her breath grew short and quick, and she had to keep it back for fear the young Hebrew might hear it. Now and then a wave higher than the rest covered her open lips with spray, wet her hair, and even touched the robe twisted around her head. Happily for her, as her strength was almost exhausted, they soon reached calmer water. A bundle of reeds floating down the stream grazed her as it passed, and frightened her terribly. This dark green mass, in the obscurity, looked like the back of a crocodile: Ta-

hoser fancied that she had felt the rough hide of the
monster, but she recovered from her fright, and,
swimming onward, murmured to herself,—

"What does it matter if the crocodiles devour me,
if Poëri does not love me?"

The danger was real, above all at night.   During
the day the perpetual running to and fro of the boats,
the work upon the quays, the noises of the town,
kept away the crocodiles, that seek the haunts least
frequented by man, to wallow in the mud and bask
in the sun ; but darkness made them bold again.

Tahoser had not thought of them.   Love does not
stop to calculate.   If the idea of this peril had presented itself to her, she would have braved it, she
who was so timid, too, that she was terrified when a
pertinacious butterfly circled around her, mistaking
her for a flower.

Suddenly the boat stopped, although the shore was
still at some distance.   Poëri rested upon the oar and
seemed to be looking about him anxiously.   He had
seen the white spot upon the water made by Tahoser's
turban.

Believing herself discovered, the intrepid swimmer
dived bravely, determined not to rise again, even
if she were suffocating, till Poëri's suspicions were
quieted.

"I was sure that some one was swimming after
me," muttered Poëri, beginning to row again.   "But
who would risk themselves in the Nile at this hour?
I must have been mad.   I mistook a cluster of white

lotus-flowers for a human head wrapped in linen; or
perhaps it was only a bit of froth, for I do not see
anything now."

When Tahoser, whose veins surged in her temples,
and who began to see red objects moving in the dark
water of the river, rose hastily to fill her lungs with
a deep breath, the shell of papyrus was moving
steadily on its way, and Poëri was using the paddle
with all the imperturbable phlegm of the allegorical
figures managing the *baris* of Maüt in the paintings
and bas-reliefs of the temples.

The shore was now only a few strokes off; the
gigantic shadows of the pylons and tremendous walls
of the Northern palace, whose opaque masses, surmounted by the points of six obelisks, stood out
against the violet background of the night and
spread in all their breadth over the stream, protecting Tahoser, who could swim now without fear of
being seen.

Poëri landed a little beyond the palace on his way
down the Nile, fastening the boat to a stake so that
he might find it on his return : then he took up his
palm-stick and hastily mounted the steps of the quay.

Poor Tahoser, nearly exhausted, grasped the first
step of the staircase, and drew from the water with
difficulty her streaming limbs, that seemed to grow
tired and stiff all at once on being exposed to the
air ; but she had accomplished the hardest part of
her task.

She ascended the flight of steps with one hand

upon her heart, which was beating violently, and the other holding the wet robe wound about her head. After observing the direction that Poëri had taken, she sat down on the upper step, undid her tunic, and put it on again. The contact of the damp stuff made a slight chill run through her.

The night was mild, too, and the wind was blowing warm from the south, but fatigue made her feverish, and her little teeth chattered : she summoned together all her energies, and, edging along the sloping walls of the enormous structures, succeeded in not losing sight of the young Hebrew, who, turning the corner of the immense brick enclosure about the palace, made his way across the streets of Thebes.

After a quarter of an hour's walk, palaces, temples, and grand dwellings disappeared, giving place to humbler habitations ; granite, limestone, and sandstone were followed by crude brick, and clay mixed with straw.

Architectural forms were effaced, hovels rose up here and there like blisters or excrescences, in isolated spots, and out of the midst of straggling vegetation, filling the darkness with monstrous shapes ; sticks of wood, and bricks, lying in heaps, obstructed the way.

Out of the silence proceeded strange sounds : an owl darted through the air with noiseless wing ; lean dogs lifted their long pointed muzzles in the air, following with plaintive howls the irregular flight of bats ; and scarabœi and timid reptiles ran over the dry grass, making it rustle.

"What if Harphré told the truth after all?" thought Tahoser, impressed by the sinister aspect of the place. "Can Poëri be coming here to sacrifice a child to those barbarous gods that love blood and suffering? If so, there never was a place better suited to such cruel rites."

However, taking advantage of shady corners, angles of walls, occasional bushes, and uneven ground, she managed to keep always at about the same distance from Poëri.

"If I have to assist, as an invisible witness, at some scene horrible as a nightmare, listen to the cries of the victim, and see the sacrificer tear out with his bloody hands the smoking heart from the little body, I will go on to the end," said Tahoser to herself, as she watched the young Hebrew enter a clay hut, through whose cracks a yellow light was shining.

When Poëri had gone in, the daughter of Petamounoph drew near, no pebble grating under her phantom-like step, and no dog barking to notify any one of her presence. She walked around the hut, trying to still her throbbing heart, and holding her breath, until she discovered, by its gleam in the dark clay wall, an opening large enough to see into the interior.

The room, less humble than one might have supposed from the appearance of the hovel, was lighted

14

by a little lamp; the smooth walls had the polish of stucco. On wooden pedestals painted with different colors stood gold and silver vases; jewels sparkled in open cases; plates of brilliant metal blazed upon the walls, and a bouquet of flowers filled a jar of enamelled ware placed upon a little table in the centre of the room.

But it was not the details of the interior that interested Tahoser, although the contrast of this hidden luxury with the miserable appearance of things outside had caused her some surprise at first. Her attention was irresistibly drawn towards another object.

Upon a raised flooring covered with mats sat a marvellously beautiful woman of some unknown race. She was fairer than any of the daughters of Egypt, fair as a lily, white as milk, white as the lambs when they come up from being washed; her eyebrows were like bows of ebony, the ends meeting over a delicate aquiline nose with nostrils tinted like the pink lining of a sea-shell. She had the eyes of a dove, brilliant and gentle at the same time; her lips were little crimson bands showing a glint of pearl between; her hair hung either side of her pome-granate cheeks in clusters, lustrous and black as two bunches of ripe grapes; pendants trembled in her ears, and necklaces of gold with silver-incrusted coins attached, sparkled about her throat, round and polished as a column of alabaster.

Her dress was singular: it consisted of a wide

tunic, embroidered with stripes and pleasing designs in different colors, descending from the shoulders to the middle of the leg, and leaving the arms bare.

The young Hebrew sat near her on the mat, carrying on a conversation with her, the letter of which was unintelligible to Tahoser, though the meaning was plain enough to disturb her peace of mind ; for Poëri and Rachel were expressing themselves in their native tongue, so sweet always to the exile and the captive.

It is hard to destroy hope when one is in love.

"Perhaps it is his sister," said Tahoser to herself, "and he has come to visit her in secret, so that no one may discover that he belongs to this captive nation."

Then she put her face to the crevice, listening with painful intensity to the harmonious and flowing words, every syllable of which contained a secret that she would have given her life to know, but they were only vague and elusive utterances, meaningless to her as the wind among the trees and the waves upon the shore.

"She is very beautiful—for a sister," she murmured, devouring with a jealous eye this strange and charming face, with its fair skin and red lips, whose beauty, heightened by the foreign ornaments, had something fatal about it.

"Oh, Rachel! My beloved Rachel!" repeated Poëri, again and again.

Tahoser remembered having heard him murmur

these words while she fanned and soothed his slumber.

"He even thought of her in his sleep: Rachel, no doubt, is her name." And the poor child felt a sharp pang in her breast, as if all the uræi-serpents of the entablatures, all the asps of the Pharaonic crowns, had set their venomous fangs in her heart.

Rachel laid her head on Poëri's shoulder, like a flower drooping with its burden of fragrance and love; the young man's lips brushed the tresses of the beautiful Jewess, who leaned back languidly, offering her fair brow and half-closed eyes to this timid and entreating caress; then their hands met, clasping each other tenderly.

"Oh that I had surprised him at some impious and dreadful rite, cutting the throat of some human victim with his own hands, drinking the blood from a black earthen cup, and rubbing his face in it! It seems to me that I could have borne it better than to see him embrace this beautiful woman so timidly," faltered Tahoser, in a faint voice, as she sank upon the ground in the shadow of the hut.

Twice she tried to rise again, but she fell upon her knees: a mist came before her eyes, her limbs relaxed, and she lost consciousness.

In the mean time Poëri left the hut, giving Rachel a parting kiss.

CHAPTER X.

PHARAOH, anxious and furious on account of the disappearance of Tahoser, had yielded to that longing for a change of scene that takes possession of the heart when it is tortured by an ungratified passion. To the great chagrin of Amensé, Hont-Reché, and Twéa, his favorites, who had employed all the arts of feminine coquetry in their endeavors to keep him at the summer pavilion, he had taken up his abode in the Northern palace, on the opposite shore of the Nile.

In his morose state of mind, it annoyed him to have his women around him and to hear them chatter. All that was not Tahoser was distasteful to him: these beauties that he had once thought so fascinating now appeared ugly in his sight; their young forms, so lithe and graceful, that fell into such voluptuous poses, their long eyes, made brighter with antimony and sparkling with desire, their crimson lips, wreathed in languishing smiles, revealing their white teeth,— everything about them, even to the sweet fragrance emanating from the fresh skin as from a bouquet of flowers or box of perfume, had become odious and intolerable to him: he could not forgive them for having loved them, and it was a mystery to him how he had ever found any attraction in such vulgar charms. When Twéa touched his breast with her

l　　14*

pink tapering fingers, trembling with emotion, as if
to remind him of the familiarity of former times,
when Hont-Reché placed before him the checker-
board supported upon two lions set back to back,
offering herself as his opponent, or Amensé, in a respectful and beseeching manner, presented him with
a lotus-flower, he could scarcely refrain from striking
them with his sceptre, and his hawk-like eyes darted
forth such contemptuous glances that the poor women
who had shown such temerity retired in confusion,
and, their eyelids wet with tears, leaned mutely against
the painted walls, striving to sink quietly out of sight
among the figures in the frescoes.

To avoid these scenes full of emotion and tears,
he withdrew to his Theban palace, gloomy and silent;
and there, instead of remaining seated upon his
throne in the solemn attitude of the gods and the
kings, who, having authority over all, never move,
nor lift a finger, he paced his immense rooms in a
feverish manner.

It was a curious spectacle to see this Pharaoh, tall,
imposing, and formidable as his own colossal granite
statues, making the great slabs re-echo under the
curved soles of his sandals.

As he passed them, the terrified guards seemed to
turn into stone; they ceased breathing, and you could
not even see the ostrich plumes flutter upon their
casques.

When he was at a distance again, they scarcely
dared to ask each other,—

"What is the matter with Pharaoh to-day? If he had returned worsted from his expedition, he could not be more taciturn and gloomy."

If, instead of having gained ten victories, killed twenty thousand enemies, brought back two thousand maidens chosen among the fairest, a hundred-weight of gold-dust, a thousand-weight of ebony wood and elephant tusks, without counting all the rare productions and strange animals, Pharaoh had seen his army routed, his war-chariots overturned and broken to pieces, and had escaped alone from the defeat, in the midst of a shower of arrows, covered with blood and dust, and wrenching the reins from the hands of his charioteer slain beside him, he could not have worn a more dismal and desperate look.

After all, the land of Egypt swarmed with soldiers, innumerable horses whinnied and pawed the ground in the palace stables, and the mechanics could soon have bent the wood, melted the copper, and sharpened the brass. The fortune of war changes; a disaster is soon repaired. But to express a wish that could not be gratified upon the spot, to encounter an obstacle between his will and the accomplishment thereof, to launch a desire like a javelin and have it miss the mark,—this was what had astounded Pharaoh in the lofty regions of his omnipotence. For an instant the idea occurred to him that he was but a man! He wandered into the vast courts, along the dromos of gigantic columns, passing beneath the huge pylons, between the obelisks shooting up here and there, and the colossi that gazed at him with great wondering eyes; he entered the hypostyle hall, losing himself in the granite forest of its hundred and sixty-two pillars, high and strong as towers. The faces of the gods, the kings, and allegorical personages, painted upon the walls, seemed to turn towards him the full eye inscribed in black lines upon their profiles, the uroei-serpents to writhe and inflate their throats, the divinities with the head of an ibis to stretch out their necks, the globes to lift their wings of stone from the cornices and move them up and down. These odd representations appeared to live and breathe in a curious and fantastic manner, peopling with an appearance of life the solitude of the enormous room, as large itself as a whole palace.

These divinities, ancestors, and chimerical creations were startled out of their eternal immobility to see Pharaoh, generally as calm as they, moving to and fro as though his body were made of flesh, and not of porphyry or basalt.

Weary of wandering about in this grove of columns sustaining a sky of granite, like a lion running his wrinkled muzzle over the light sands of the desert in search of prey, Pharaoh mounted the terraced roof of the palace, and, stretching himself on a low couch, had Timopht summoned to his side.

Timopht appeared and advanced from the head of the staircase to the place where Pharaoh was lying, prostrating himself at every step. He feared the wrath of the master whose favor for a moment he had hoped to gain. Would his ingenuity in discovering Tahoser's dwelling prove a sufficient excuse for the crime of having lost all trace of the beautiful girl? Raising one knee, and resting upon the other, Timopht extended his hands in supplication to the king.

"O king, do not have me killed, or too severely beaten : the beautiful Tahoser, daughter of Petamounoph, upon whom your longing glance has deigned to descend, as the hawk darts upon the dove, will undoubtedly be found again ; and when she returns to her house and sees your magnificent gifts, her heart will be touched, and she will come of her own accord and take the place you may assign to her among the women of your gynecæum."

"Have you questioned the servants and slaves ?" demanded Pharaoh. "The rod loosens the most stubborn tongues, and suffering wrings from people what they want to hide."

"Nofré and Souhem, her favorite attendant and oldest slave, told me they had discovered that the bolts of the garden-gate had been drawn, and probably their mistress had gone out in that direction. The gate opens on the river, and the water does not keep the track of the boats."

"What did the boatmen of the Nile say ?"

"They had seen nothing ; only one of them said that a woman, poorly clad, had gone over very early.

But it could not have been the rich and beautiful
Tahoser, whose face you remarked, and who walks
like a queen in her elegant garments."

Pharaoh did not seem to be convinced by Timopht's argument; he leaned his chin in the palm of
his hand and mused awhile. Poor Timopht waited
in silence, dreading an explosion of wrath. The
king's lips moved as though he were talking to himself:

" That mean dress was a disguise. Yes, that was
it. Thus attired, she passed over to the other side.
That Timopht is an idiot, without the least penetra-
tion. I have a great mind to have him thrown
to the crocodiles or soundly thrashed. But what
could have been her motive? A young girl of high
birth, daughter of a chief priest, to run away from
her palace, alone, without informing any one of her
plans! Perhaps there is some love-affair at the
bottom of it all."

At this thought Pharaoh's visage grew scarlet, as
if the flame of a fire were reflected in it: all the
blood in his body mounted to his face; a frightful
pallor succeeded this flush, his eyebrows twitched
convulsively like the serpents upon his diadems, his
mouth contracted, his teeth gritted together, and his
whole physiognomy became so appalling that Timopht, horror-stricken, rolled over on his face upon
the slabs like a dead man.

But Pharaoh grew calm again; his face resumed
its unruffled, bored, and majestic air; and, seeing

that Timopht did not move, he pushed him disdain-
fully with his foot. When Timopht, who saw himself
already laid out upon the funeral bier with jackals'
feet, his side gaping open, his bowels gone, and his
body ready to be plunged into the natron bath, got
up, he did not venture to raise his eyes to the king,
but remained squatting upon his heels, his mind a
prey to the keenest anguish.

"Come, Timopht," said his majesty, "get up,
and despatch emissaries in all directions; have the
temples, palaces, houses, villas, gardens, and even
the humblest cabins, searched, so that we may find
Tahoser; send out chariots over all the roads, have
the Nile traversed in every direction; go yourself,
and ask of every one you meet whether they have
seen a woman answering to this description; violate
the sacredness of the tombs if she has sought to hide
herself in the asylum of the dead, in the heart of
some syrinx or burial-chamber. Search for her as
Isis sought for her husband Osiris, torn to pieces by
a Typhon, and bring her to me dead or alive, or, by
the serpent of my pshent, and by the lotus-bud of
my sceptre, you shall die under the most frightful
torture."

Timopht darted off with the speed of an ibex to
execute the mandates of Pharaoh, who, once more
tranquil, assumed one of those attitudes of severe
grandeur that the sculptors love to give to the colossi seated at the gates of the temples and palaces,
and waited dispassionately, as becomes those whose

sandals, bearing the figures of slaves bound by the elbows, rest upon the heads of nations.

A muffled rumbling resounded through the palace, and, if the sky had not been of an unchangeable lapis-lazuli, one might have thought a storm were brewing: it was the noise made by the chariots dashing off at a gallop in all directions, their rapid wheels thundering over the stones.

Soon Pharaoh could see, from the top of the terrace, boats dividing the water under the powerful strokes of the rowers, and his emissaries starting out upon the other shore across the country.

The Libyan range, with its rosy lights and sapphire shadows, stretched along the horizon, serving as a background to the gigantic buildings of Rameses, Amenoph, and Menephta; the pylons with sloping angles, the walls with concave cornices, the colossi with their hands upon their knees, stood out in relief with the golden sunlight streaming over them, losing none of their grandeur in the distance. But Pharaoh was not looking at these proud structures: among the groups of palms, and in the midst of cultivated grounds, houses and painted kiosks rose here and there, in patches upon the brilliant green of the vegetation. Under one of those roofs, beneath one of those terraces, Tahoser was undoubtedly concealed, and he would have liked, through some magical means, to have raised them up or rendered them transparent.

The hours went by; already the sun had disappeared behind the mountains, casting a final glow

over Thebes, and yet the messengers had not returned.
Pharaoh was still in the same motionless attitude.
Night had descended upon the city, calm, fresh, and
blue; the stars began to sparkle and blink their long
golden lashes in the azure depths; and the black
outlines of the silent, impassible Pharaoh loomed up
from the corner of the terrace, like a statue of basalt
cemented to the entablature. Often the night-birds
circled around his head as if about to alight; but,
frightened by his deep and regular breathing, they
flew away, flapping their wings.

From this height the king could overlook the city
stretching out at his feet. Out of the midst of the
blue shadows sprang the obelisks with pyramidal
points, the pylons, gigantic gateways traversed by
beams, high cornices, the colossi with their shoulders
above the confusion of structures, the propylons, the
columns with capitals resembling enormous granite
flowers, angles of temples and palaces revealed by
silvery touches of light; the sacred ponds spread
themselves out like mirrors of polished metal, the
sphinxes and criosphinxes squatted upon their
haunches in rows along the avenues with their paws
outstretched, and the flat roofs followed each other
in endless succession, turning white under the moon
in masses widely separated by squares and streets;
red points twinkled in the blue obscurity, as if the
stars had let some sparks fall to the ground: they
were the lamps of those still awake in the sleeping
city; farther off, between the edifices that were not

so crowded, vague groups of palms waved their leafy fans; beyond this, contours and shapes were lost in the misty immensity, for the eye of the eagle itself could not penetrate as far as the limits of Thebes, and on the other side old Hopi-Mou flowed majestically towards the sea.

Measuring with the eye and the thought this boundless city, of which he was absolute master, Pharaoh mused disconsolately on the limits of human power, and his desire gnawed at his heart like a hungry vulture. He said to himself, "All of these houses contain beings who, at sight of me, bow their heads in the dust, and who look upon my wishes as commands of the gods. When I pass, mounted upon my gilded chariot or seated in my palanquin, borne by the oëris, the hearts of the maidens beat fast as they follow me with their modest longing glances; the priests burn incense in their amschirs before me; the people wave palm-branches, and scatter flowers in my path; the whistling of one of my arrows makes nations tremble, and there is scarcely room enough upon the pylons, though they are like great perpendicular mountains, for the accounts of my victories; the quarries are nearly exhausted furnishing granite for my colossal statues; yet the time has come, in my superb satiety, when I have expressed a wish that cannot be realized! Timopht does not return : probably he has not found any clue. O Tahoser, Tahoser, how much happiness I deserve for this suspense !"

In the mean time, the emissaries, with Timopht at their head, searched the houses and scoured the country, trying to get tidings of the daughter of the priest: they even described her to the travellers they met. But no one could tell them anything. The first messenger appeared upon the terrace, announcing to Pharaoh that Tahoser was not to be found.

Pharaoh reached forth his sceptre, and the messenger fell dead, in spite of the proverbial hardness of the Egyptian skull.

A second arrived; his foot struck against the dead body of his comrade stretched upon the stone roof; a trembling seized him, for he saw that Pharaoh was angry.

"And Tahoser?" said Pharaoh, never changing his posture.

"O king! all trace of her is lost," replied the poor wretch, kneeling in the darkness before this black spectre, more like a statue of Osiris than a living king.

The motionless figure extended its granite-like arm, and the metal sceptre descended like a thunderbolt.

The second messenger rolled over beside the first.

A third met with the same fate.

Going from house to house, Timopht at last reached the pavilion of Poëri, who had been surprised that morning, upon his return from his night's excursion, to find that the pretended Hora was missing. Harphré and the other servants, who had eaten supper with her the night before, did not know what had become of her; she was not in her room, and they sought for her in vain in the gardens, wine-cellars, granaries, and bathing-places.

To the inquiries of Timopht, Poëri replied that a young girl had indeed presented herself in a supplicating attitude upon his threshold, imploring hospitality on her knees; that he had received her kindly, offering what his house afforded, but that she had departed in a mysterious manner, for what reason he could not imagine. What direction had she taken? He did not know. No doubt, somewhat rested, she had continued on her way towards the end of her journey. She was beautiful, sad, plainly dressed, and seemed to be poor. Could the name of Tahoser have been concealed under that of Hora? He would leave it to the sagacity of Timopht to decide the question.

Furnished with this information, Timopht returned to the palace, and, keeping out of the reach of Pharaoh's sceptre, related to him what he had heard.

"Why did she go to Poëri?" said Pharaoh to himself. " If Tahoser was concealed under the disguise of Hora, she loves Poëri. No, or else she would not have fled in that manner after she had been received under his roof. Ah! I will find her again, if I overturn Egypt from the cataracts to the Delta."

CHAPTER XI.

RACHEL, who, from the door-sill of the cabin, was watching Poëri as he disappeared in the distance, thought that she heard a faint sigh; she listened.

The dogs were baying at the moon, an owl hooted dismally, and the crocodiles, among the reeds in the river, imitated, with their cries, the voice of a child in distress.

The young Israelite was about to enter again, when a more distinct moan, that she could not mistake for the sounds peculiar to the night, and that evidently issued from a human breast, struck her ear a second time.

She walked cautiously, fearing some treachery, towards the spot whence the sound proceeded, and perceived in the transparent blue shadow something resembling a human form stretched upon the ground; the wet drapery clung to the figure of the feigned Hora, and, revealing her pure rounded outlines, betrayed her sex. Rachel, seeing that she had nothing more serious before her than a woman in a swoon, lost all fear, and knelt down beside her, to listen to her breathing and the beating of her heart. One expired upon her white lips, the other barely lifted her cold bosom. Feeling the water with

15*

which the stranger's dress was soaked, Rachel thought at first that it was blood, and imagined that the victim of a murder lay before her: so, in order to render all the aid possible, she called Tamar, her servant, and between them they carried Tahoser into the cabin.

The two women laid her upon the couch. Tamar held up the lamp, while Rachel bent over the young girl, searching for the wound; but no red gash stained the waxen pallor of Tahoser's skin, and her robe had no crimson spots upon it. They took off the wet garment and threw over her a striped woollen stuff, whose agreeable warmth soon restored the suspended circulation of the blood. Tahoser slowly unclosed her eyes, and looked about her in a startled manner like a captured gazelle.

It took her some time to collect her scattered thoughts. She could not yet comprehend how she had found her way into this room, upon this lounge, where, a little while ago, she had seen Poëri and the young Jewess seated beside each other, murmuring their love with hands interlocked, while she, breathless, beside herself, peered through the crack in the wall; but soon memory returned, and with it a consciousness of the situation.

The light shone directly upon Rachel's face, and Tahoser studied it in silence, grieved to find it so regular in its beauty. In vain, with all the bitterness of feminine jealousy, she tried to find some imperfection: she felt herself not surpassed,

but equalled; Rachel was the ideal Israelite, as
Tahoser was the ideal Egyptian. Hard as it was
for an interested heart, she was compelled to admit that Poëri's affection was justifiable and well
placed.

Those eyes with curving black lashes, that nose
of such a noble form, those red lips with their fascinating smile, that long and elegant oval of the face,
those arms so well developed at the shoulders and
ending in the hands of a child, that throat round
and plump, that in turning made folds more beautiful than necklaces of precious stones,—all of this, set
off with curious foreign ornaments, could not fail to
please.

"It was a great mistake on my part," said Tahoser
in her own mind, "to present myself before Poëri
in the humble garb of a supplicant, trusting to charms
too highly praised by flatterers. What folly! It
was like a soldier going into battle without cuirass
or falchion. If I had appeared surrounded by all
my luxury, covered with jewels and enamels, mounted
upon my gilded chariot, attended by my numerous
slaves, I might have touched his pride, if not his
heart."

"How do you feel now?" inquired Rachel of
Tahoser, in the Egyptian tongue, for, from the contour of the face and the arrangement of the hair in
fine braids, she had discovered that the young girl
did not belong to the Hebrew race.

The tones of her voice were gentle and compassionate, and the foreign accent made them still more charming.

Tahoser was touched in spite of herself, and replied,—

"I feel a little better: your kind care will soon restore me."

"Do not tire yourself talking," said the Jewess, placing her hand upon Tahoser's lips. "Try to sleep and recover your strength: Tamar and I will watch over your slumber."

Her emotions, the swimming across the Nile, the long journey into the deserted quarters of Thebes, had exhausted the daughter of Petamounoph. Her delicate body was worn out, and soon the long lashes drooped until they formed a dark semicircle upon the cheeks flushed with fever.

Sleep came, but it was anxious, disturbed, and full of strange dreams peopled with terrifying hallucinations: the sleeper started nervously, and disconnected words in answer to some secret dialogue of her dream fell from her parted lips.

Seated near the head of the couch, Rachel followed the changes of expression in Tahoser's face, distressed when she saw it contract with pain, and reassured when she seemed to be at ease again. Tamar, squatting down at her mistress's feet, also watched the daughter of the priest, but with a less kindly look. Vulgar instincts had set their seal upon the lines of her low forehead encircled with the wide band of the Hebrew head-dress; her eyes, brilliant yet

in spite of her age, sparkled with inquisitiveness in
their brown wrinkled sockets; her bony nose, bent
and shining as the beak of a hawk, seemed to scent
a mystery in the air, and her lips moved slightly, as
if she were framing questions.

This stranger, picked up at the threshold of the
cabin, excited her curiosity to the utmost. Where
could she have come from? How did she get there?
What had been her object? And who could she
be? Such were the questions suggesting themselves
to Tamar's mind, to which, to her great regret, she
could find no satisfactory answer.

It must be confessed, too, that Tamar, like all old
hags, hated beauty; and, on account of this, felt an
aversion for Tahoser.

The devoted servant pardoned no one but her mistress for being handsome: that beauty she considered
her own property, and she was proud and jealous
of it. Seeing that Rachel remained silent, the old
woman rose, came and sat near her, and, blinking
her eyes, whose bistre-colored lids rose and fell like
a bat's wings, said, in a low tone, in the Hebrew
tongue,—

"Mistress, the presence of this woman here bodes
no good."

"And why so, Tamar?" asked Rachel, in the
same language, and also in a low voice.

"It is strange," remarked the suspicious Tamar,
"that she should faint away just at this spot and
nowhere else."

m

"She fell at the spot where the faintness overcame her."

The old woman shook her head incredulously.

"Do you imagine," said Poëri's betrothed, "that this swoon was not genuine? A parischite might have opened her side with a sharp stone, so much did she resemble a corpse. That dead appearance of the eye, those white lips, colorless cheeks, and lifeless limbs, as well as the coldness of the skin, so like death, could not have been feigned."

"No, of course not," rejoined Tamar; "though there are women clever enough to employ all of these symptoms to gain their point, and in such an artful manner as to deceive the wisest. I think, however, that the young girl did really faint away."

"Then upon what do you base your suspicions?"

"How did she find her way in the middle of the night into this remote quarter, inhabited only by the poor captives of our tribe, whom the wicked Pharaoh employs at making bricks without giving them any straw to bake their clay when it is moulded? What motive led this Egyptian into the neighborhood of our poor hovels? And why was her dress as wet as if she had been in a pond, or in the river?"

"I cannot tell, any more than you."

"What if it were one of the spies of our masters?" said the old woman, in whose keen eyes gleamed a spark of hate. "Great things are in the course of preparation : who knows but that the alarm may have been given?"

"How could this sick girl injure us? She is in our power, alone, weak, helpless, and incapable even of moving now; and, besides, if there were anything suspicious about her we could keep her prisoner until the day of the exodus."

"At all events, do not trust her: see how delicate and soft her hands are." And old Tamar lifted one of the arms of the sleeping Tahoser.

"How can the delicacy of her skin make her dangerous?"

"Oh, the imprudence of youth!" exclaimed Tamar. "Oh, the madness of youth! that sees only so far, that walks through life full of confidence, with no faith in ambushes, in briers in the grass or fire under the ashes, and that would be ready to handle an asp, believing it to be a harmless snake! Try to be reasonable, Rachel, and to keep your eyes open. This woman is not of the class to which she pretends to belong: her thumb has not been flattened with the thread of the spindle; and that small hand, softened with ointments and perfumes, has never worked: this appearance of poverty is only a disguise."

Tamar's words seemed to make an impression upon Rachel, and she examined Tahoser more closely.

The lamp shed its trembling rays over her, and, in the yellow light, the pure outlines of the priest's daughter stood out in all the abandonment of sleep. The arm that Tamar had lifted lay once more upon the striped woollen covering, looking still fairer in

contrast with the dark stuff; the wrist was clasped
by the bracelet of sandal-wood, cheap ornament of
a coquetry that could not afford anything more
costly, but if the ornament were rude and poorly
carved, the flesh really seemed to have been kneaded
in the perfumed baths of the rich. Rachel observed,
also, that Tahoser was comely; but this discovery
did not arouse any unkindly feelings in her heart.
This beauty softened instead of irritating her, as it
did Tamar. She could not believe that such perfection enclosed a base and treacherous soul, and
in this instance her youthful ingenuousness judged
more correctly than the aged experience of her attendant. Day appeared at last, and Tahoser's fever
increased ; she had moments of delirium followed by
prolonged slumber.

"If she should die here," said Tamar, "they
would accuse us of having murdered her."

"She will not die," replied Rachel, holding a
cup of fresh water to the sick girl's lips, that were
parched with fever.

"I would go to the Nile at night and throw her
body into it," continued the obstinate Tamar, "and
the crocodiles would soon make away with it."

The day passed, night fell, and at the accustomed
hour Poëri, having made the usual signal, appeared,
as on the evening previous, in the door-way of the
cabin. Rachel went to meet him with her finger
upon her lips, cautioning him to be quiet, and to
speak in a low tone, as Tahoser was sleeping.

Poëri, whom Rachel took by the hand, to lead
him to the lounge where Tahoser was lying, immediately recognized the pretended Hora, whose disappearance had been upon his mind, especially since
the visit of Timopht, who was searching for her in
his master's name.

A profound amazement was depicted in his face
when he rose up after having leaned over the bed to
assure himself whether it was indeed the young girl
whom he had taken under his roof, for he could not
conceive how she had found her way to this spot.

This look of surprise went to Rachel's heart; she
placed herself in front of Poëri so as to read the
truth in his eyes, laid her hands upon his shoulders,
and, giving him a searching glance, demanded in a
dry, abrupt manner, in strong contrast to her usual
tones, that resembled the cooing of a dove,—

" You know her, then?"

Tamar's face wore a satisfied grimace: she was
proud of her discernment, and almost glad to find
her suspicions respecting the stranger confirmed.

" Yes," responded Poëri, frankly.

The burning eyes of the servant sparkled with
malicious curiosity.

Rachel's countenance resumed its expression of
trust; she no longer doubted her lover.

Poeri explained to her that a young girl had presented herself before him, under the name of Hora,
imploring assistance; that he had extended the
hospitality one cannot refuse; that the next day

she was missing among his servants, and that he could not imagine how she had found her way there. He added that the emissaries of Pharaoh were in search of Tahoser, the daughter of the high-priest Petamounoph, who had disappeared from her palace.

"You see that I was right, mistress," exclaimed Tamar, triumphantly : " Hora and Tahoser are the same person."

" It may be," replied Poëri ; " but there are several mysteries that I cannot fathom. First of all, why Tahoser (if it is she) should have adopted this disguise? And by what miracle do I find in this spot a young girl whom I left yesterday evening on the other side of the river, and who certainly did not know where I was going ?"

" She must have followed you," replied Rachel.

" I am sure that there was no boat upon the river at that hour but my own."

" That accounts for her hair streaming with water and her dress being drenched : she undoubtedly swam across the Nile."

" Indeed, it seemed to me once that I saw something resembling a human head above the water."

"It was hers,—poor child," said Rachel : "her swoon and her exhaustion prove it ; for, after your departure, I found her lying unconscious outside of the cabin, and brought her in."

" All must have happened as you represent," replied the young man. " I see my way clearly to the facts of the case now, but I cannot comprehend the motives."

" I can explain them to you," responded Rachel, smiling, " although I am a poor ignorant girl, and you have been compared, on account of your knowledge, to the priests of Egypt, who study day and night, buried away in their cells, covered with mysterious hieroglyphics, whose meaning they alone can interpret ; but sometimes men who are so occupied with astronomy, music, and mathematics cannot divine what is passing in the head of a young girl. They will discern a distant star in space and pass over a heart within their reach. Hora, or rather Tahoser, for it is she, assumed this disguise in order to introduce herself into your house and to live beside you. Prompted by jealousy, she followed you in the dark, and, at the risk of being devoured by the crocodiles in the river, swam the Nile. Having reached this spot, she watched us through a crack in the wall, and could not endure the spectacle of our happiness. She loves you, because you are very handsome, very strong, and very gentle ; but I do not mind it, since you do not care for her. Do you understand now ?"

A faint blush suffused Poëri's cheeks : he feared that Rachel might be displeased, and that she only talked in this way to try him ; but Rachel's pure and limpid glance was free from any *arrière-pensée.* She did not hate Tahoser for loving the one whom she also loved.

Amid the phantoms of her dreams Tahoser perceived Poëri standing beside her. An ecstatic joy illuminated her face, and, half rising, she seized the young man's hand and carried it to her lips.

" Her lips burn," said Poëri, withdrawing his hand.

" Love has as much to do with it as fever," replied Rachel ; " but she is quite ill : what if Tamar were to go and bring Moses here? He knows more than all of Pharaoh's magicians, whose miracles he can imitate ; he knows the healing virtues of plants, and can make potions from them that would revive the dead : he will cure Tahoser, for I am not cruel enough to wish her to die."

Tamar went off with a crabbed countenance, and soon returned, followed by a venerable man of tall stature, whose majestic air commanded respect ; an immense white beard descended in waves to his breast, and on either side of his forehead rose two enormous protuberances shining with light: they were like horns or rays. Beneath his thick brows his eyes darted flames. In spite of his simple garments, he looked like a prophet or a god.

After Poëri had explained matters, he sat down by Tahoser's couch, and, stretching out his hands over her, said,—

" In the name of Him who is omnipotent, and beside whom all other gods are but idols and devils, though you do not belong to the chosen race of the Lord, damsel, be healed !"

CHAPTER XII.

THE majestic old man retired with a slow and solemn step, leaving a light, as it were, in his path. Tahoser, surprised to find her illness disappear so suddenly, looked around the room, and in a few moments, wrapping about her the stuff that the young Jewess had thrown over her, she slid her feet down to the ground and sat up on the edge of the couch. Her exhaustion and her fever had entirely vanished. She was as fresh as if she had just awakened from a long sleep, and her beauty shone forth in all its purity.

Putting the braided masses of hair behind her ears with her little hands, she disclosed to view a countenance radiant with love, as if she longed to have Poëri read therein. But seeing that he remained at Rachel's side without moving, or giving her the slightest encouragement by word or sign, she rose slowly, and, approaching the young Jewess, threw her arms despairingly about her neck.

She remained thus, with her face hidden upon Rachel's breast, her hot tears flowing in silence.

Sometimes a sob that she could not repress made her tremble convulsively upon her rival's bosom. This complete surrender, this frank expression of sorrow, touched Rachel: Tahoser acknowledged herself

16*

vanquished, and implored her sympathy with mute entreaty, appealing to her generosity as a woman.

Rachel, agitated, embraced her, and said, "Dry your tears, and do not grieve in this manner. You love Poëri; well, continue to love him: I shall not be jealous. Jacob, a patriarch of our race, had two wives: one was called Rachel, like myself, the other Leah; Jacob preferred Rachel, and yet Leah, who had not your beauty, lived happily beside him."

Tahoser knelt at Rachel's feet and kissed her hands; Rachel lifted her up and clasped her in her arms.

These two women, summing up in their persons all the beauty of their respective races, formed a charming group: Tahoser, elegant, finely made, and graceful, like a child that has grown up too rapidly; Rachel, dazzling, large, and superb in her precocious maturity.

"Tahoser," said Poëri, "for that is your name, I believe?—Tahoser, daughter of the high-priest Peta-mounoph——"

The young girl made a sign of assent.

"How does it happen that you, who dwell in a rich palace in Thebes, surrounded by slaves, with the handsomest Egyptians at your feet, have set your affections upon the son of an enslaved people, a stranger who has no part in your religion, and who is in every way so far separated from you?"

Rachel and Tahoser smiled, and the daughter of the high-priest replied,—

"It is for this reason alone."

"Although I find favor in Pharaoh's sight, am steward of his domains and wear the gilded ram's horns at the agricultural fêtes, yet I cannot rise to your station; in the eyes of the Egyptians I am only a slave, and you belong to the highest and most venerated order of the sacerdotal caste. If you love me, —and I cannot doubt it,—you will have to give up your rank——"

"Have I not already acted as your servant? Hora retained nothing belonging to Tahoser, not even her necklaces of enamels and calasiris of transparent gauze; and this is why I appeared ugly to you."

"You will have to leave your country and follow me to unknown lands, across deserts where the sun burns and the hot winds blow, where the shifting sands make all roads alike, where no tree springs up and no fountain gushes forth, among valleys of illusion and perdition, strewn with bleached bones as landmarks."

"I will go," tranquilly replied Tahoser.

"That is not all," continued Poëri: "your gods are not mine,—your gods of brass, of basalt, and of granite, fashioned by the hand of man, monstrous images with heads like hawks, apes, ibises, cows, jackals, and lions, who assume an animal-mask, as if the human face, that is a reflection of Jehovah's, embarrassed them. It is said, 'Thou shalt worship neither stone, wood, nor metal.' In those enormous temples, cemented together with the life-blood of oppressed nations, crouch impure demons, wearing a hideous grin, who usurp the libations, offerings, and sacrifices. One God alone, infinite, eternal, without form or color, suffices to fill the immensity of the heavens, which you people with a multitude of phantoms. Our God has created us, and it is you who create your gods."

Enamored as Tahoser was with Poëri, these words had a strange effect upon her, and she shrank from him in terror. Daughter of a high-priest, she was accustomed to venerate these gods that the young Hebrew spoke of in such a bold and blasphemous manner: she had offered up on their altars bouquets of lotus-flowers, and had burnt incense before their impassible images: amazed and charmed, she had wandered through their temples decorated with gorgeous paintings. She had seen her father perform the mysterious rites, had followed the colleges of priests, bearing the symbolical *baris*, through the immense propylons and the interminable avenues of sphinxes, had admired with a feeling of awe that part of *psychostasia* where the trembling soul is weighed before Osiris armed with scourge and crook, and had contemplated with dreamy eye the frescoes representing emblematic figures on their way to the occidental regions: she could not so hastily renounce her faith.

She was silent a few moments, hesitating between her religion and her love; but love was victorious, and she replied,—

"You will teach me about your God, and I will try to understand him."

"Very well," answered Poëri: "you shall be my wife. In the mean time remain here, for Pharaoh, who must be in love with you, has his emissaries out looking for you: he will not find you beneath this humble roof, and in a few days you will be beyond his power. But the night is passing, and I must go."

Poëri departed, and the two young women lay down beside each other on the little couch, and soon fell asleep, holding each other by the hand like sisters.

Tamar, who during the preceding scene had remained squatting in one corner of the room, like a bat clinging to a ledge by the hooks on its wings, now, muttering some disconnected words, and drawing down the wrinkles in her low forehead, rose to her feet, and, leaning over the bed, listened to the breathing of the slumberers. When she was convinced from its regularity that they were sleeping soundly, she went towards the door, creeping along with infinite precaution.

Outside at last, she hastened with fleet steps towards the Nile, shaking off the dogs that seized hold of her tunic, or dragging them along in the dust until they let go; again she glared at them with such fierce looks that they recoiled with plaintive howls, allowing her to pass.

She had soon crossed the dangerous wastes and deserts infested at night by the members of the association of thieves, and reached the opulent quarters of

Thebes. Three or four streets, lined with grand
edifices whose shadows were cast at immense angles,
brought her to the walls of the palace, the goal of
her journey.

It must be entered, and that was not an easy matter
at this hour of the night for an old Hebrew servant,
whose feet were gray with dust, and who was clad in
suspicious-looking rags.

She presented herself at the main pylon, guarded
by fifty criosphinxes, crouching down before it in
two rows like monsters ready to crush between their
jaws of granite any rash being who might try to
pass through.

The sentinels halted and struck her rudely with
the wooden ends of their javelins, demanding what
she wanted.

"I want to see Pharaoh," replied the old woman,
rubbing her back.

"Oh, yes!—very likely we will disturb Pharaoh,
the beloved of Amon-Ra, the favorite of Phré, and
autocrat of the nations, for such an old witch!" cried
the soldiers, holding their sides with laughter.

Tamar repeated persistently : "I must see Pharaoh
at once."

"You have chosen a favorable moment! Pharaoh
has just killed three messengers with his sceptre;
he is up yonder on the terrace, immovable, and as
sinister-looking as Typhon, the spirit of evil," said
one of the soldiers, deigning to parley with her.

Rachel's servant tried to pass the guards : the

javelins descended one after the other upon her head, like hammers on an anvil.

She began to scream like an osprey when its feathers are plucked out.

At this noise, an oëris ran forward: the soldiers stopped beating Tamar.

"What does this woman want?" demanded the oëris; "and why are you beating her?"

"I want to see Pharaoh," cried Tamar, clinging to the officer's knees.

"It is impossible," replied the oëris, "even though in place of being a poor wretch you were one of the highest dignitaries of the realm."

"I know where Tahoser is," whispered the old hag, dwelling upon each syllable.

The oëris, at these words, seized Tamar's hand, drew her through the first pylon, and led her along the avenue of columns, by the hypostyle hall, into the second court, where stood the granite sanctuary, in front of which were the two columns with lotus-flower capitals; there, calling Timopht, he handed Tamar over to him. Timopht led the servant out on the terrace where Pharaoh sat, melancholy and silent.

"Do not address him within reach of his sceptre," Timopht advised the Israelite.

As soon as she descried the king in the darkness, Tamar prostrated herself upon the slabs beside the bodies that had not been removed, then, in a few moments, raising herself again, said, in a bold tone of voice,—

" O Pharaoh, do not kill me : I bring good news."

" Speak without fear," replied the king, whose
wrath was appeased.

" I know the hiding-place of this Tahoser whom
your messengers are seeking for at the four quarters
of the wind."

At the name of Tahoser, Pharaoh rose to his feet,
and took a few steps towards the kneeling Tamar.

" If you are telling the truth, you may take from
my granite apartments all the gold and other treasures you can carry."

" I will deliver her up to you, rest assured," said
the old woman, with a harsh laugh.

What motive had induced Tamar to acquaint Pharaoh with Tahoser's place of refuge ?   She wished
to prevent a union that displeased her ; she had a
blind, unreasonable, mad, almost savage antipathy
to the Egyptian race, and the idea of breaking Tahoser's heart was delightful to her.   Once in Pharaoh's hands, Rachel's rival could not escape again :
the granite walls of the palace would know how to
guard their prey.

" Where is she ?" demanded Pharaoh.   " Point
out the place.   I must see her at once."

" Your majesty, no one but I can guide you there.
I know the windings of those out-of-the-way quarters where the humblest of your servants would
scorn to set his foot.   Tahoser is there, in a hovel
made of clay and straw, with nothing to distinguish
it from the neighboring huts, among the piles of

bricks that the Hebrews mould for you, beyond the limits of the town dwellings."

"Very well, then : I will trust to you. Timopht, prepare a chariot."

Timopht departed.

Presently the rolling of wheels over the flags of the court, and the trampling of the horses that the grooms were harnessing, could be heard.

Pharaoh descended, followed by Tamar.

He sprang into the car, took the reins, and, seeing that Tamar hesitated, "Make haste and mount," he commanded; then he clapped his tongue to the roof of his mouth, and the horses at once started off. The awakened echoes repeated the rumbling of the wheels, making a sound like distant thunder, in the silence of the night, among those high and spacious rooms.

This hideous old hag, clinging to the rim of the car with her bony fingers, beside this monarch of colossal stature and godlike mien, presented a strange spectacle, that, fortunately, was without other witness than the stars sparkling amid the blue-black fields of heaven : placed thus side by side, they resembled the evil genii of monstrous shape that accompany lost souls to hell.

"Is it in this direction?" asked Pharaoh of the servant, as they came to the end of a street branching off in opposite directions.

"Yes," replied Tamar, pointing in the right direction with her skinny hand.

The horses, urged on by the whip, dashed forward, and the chariot sprang over the stones with a clatter of brass.

All this time Tahoser slept beside Rachel, and in her sleep she had a strange vision.

It seemed to her that she was in an immense temple of granite; enormous columns of prodigious height supported a blue dome blazing with stars like the sky; innumerable rows of hieroglyphics ran up and down the length of the walls, between symbolical frescoes of a variety of brilliant tints. All the gods of Egypt were holding a rendezvous in this universal sanctuary, not in effigies of brass, basalt, or porphyry, but under a living form. In the first ranks were seated the super-celestial gods,—Knef, Bouto, Ptah, Pan-Mendes, Hathor, Phré, and Isis; after these came the twelve celestial gods,—six male deities, Rempha, Pi-Zéous, Ertosi, Pi-Hermes, Imuthés, and six female deities, the Moon, the Ether, Fire, Water, Earth, and Air. Behind them swarmed a vague and indistinguishable multitude, the three hundred and sixty-five Décans, or familiar demons of every day. Following these appeared the terrestrial divinities,—the second Osiris, Haroeri, Typhon, the second Isis, Nephthys, Anubis, with the head of a dog, Thoth, Busiris, Bubastis, and the great Serapis. Beyond, in the shade, were visible the idols in the form of animals,—bulls, crocodiles, ibises, hippopotamuses. In the middle of the temple, in an open sarcophagus, lay the priest Petamounoph, with the bandages removed from his face, looking upon the strange and monstrous assemblage with an ironical air. He was dead, yet he lived and spoke, as it often happens in dreams, and he said to his daughter,—

" Ask of them whether they are gods."

Then Tahoser went around, putting to each this question, and all of them answered,—

" We are but numbers, laws, forces, attributes, emanations, and thoughts of God, but not one of us is the true God."

Then Poëri appeared upon the threshold of the temple, and, taking Tahoser by the hand, led her towards a light so strong that beside it the sun would have appeared dim, and in the midst of it shone a triangle of unknown words.

In the mean time, Pharaoh's chariot surmounted every obstacle, and its axle-trees grazed the walls in the narrow streets.

" Curb your horses," said Tamar to Pharaoh: " the rattling of the wheels in these retired and silent quarters might give the alarm to the fugitive, and she might still escape you."

Pharaoh, finding the advice judicious, in spite of his impatience, checked the furious pace of his team.

"It is yonder," said Tamar. "I left the door open. Enter, and I will watch your horses."

The king descended from the chariot, and, bending his head, went into the cabin.

The lamp, which was still burning, shed its dying light upon the sleeping pair.

Pharaoh lifted Tahoser in his strong arms and started towards the door of the hut.

When the daughter of the priest unclosed her eyes and saw Pharaoh's beaming countenance so near her own, she thought at first that it was one of the phantoms of her dream metamorphosed; but the night-air fanning her face restored her to a consciousness of reality.

Mad with fear, she longed to cry out, to call for help; but her throat refused to utter a sound. Besides, who would come to her aid against Pharaoh?

With one bound the king sprang into his chariot; then, passing the reins around his body, and pressing the half-dead girl to his heart, he started his coursers at a gallop in the direction of the Northern palace.

Tamar, gliding like a serpent into the cabin, squatted down in her accustomed place, watching, with a glance almost as tender as that of a mother, her dear Rachel, who was still asleep.

CHAPTER XIII.

THE current of fresh air created by the rapid movement of the chariot soon revived her. Pressed and almost crushed against Pharaoh's breast by his arms of granite, there was scarcely room enough for the beating of her heart, and the hard enamels of his gorget left their impress upon her panting bosom. The horses, to which the king gave rein by leaning towards the front of the chariot, sped onward furiously; the wheels spun around, the brass scales rattled, the heated axles fairly smoked. The terrified Tahoser saw dimly, as if in a dream, flying past them on the right and left, a confusion of structures, clumps of trees, palaces, temples, pylons, obelisks, and colossi, rendered alarming and fantastic by the darkness. What thoughts were coursing through her brain during this wild ride? Her ideas had no more form than those of the trembling dove in the claws of the falcon bearing it to its nest: a mute horror stupefied her, iced her blood, and benumbed her faculties. Her limbs hung inert, her will was as powerless as her muscles, and, if Pharaoh's arms had not supported her, she would have fallen in a heap on the floor of the car like a bit of stuff when it is tossed aside. Twice she imagined that she felt a hot breath and burning lips upon her cheek: she made no effort to

turn her head aside: terror had slain her modesty.
As the chariot jarred violently against a stone, a
vague instinct of self-preservation made her grasp the
king's shoulder and cling closely to him, then, letting
go, once more she hung with all her light weight upon
the circle of flesh that was crushing her.

The equipage entered a dromos of sphinxes, at the
end of which rose a gigantic pylon surmounted by a
cornice upon which the emblematic globe spread its
wings: as it was already growing lighter, the priest's
daughter at once recognized the king's palace. Then
despair seized upon her: she struggled and tried to
free herself, pushing with her delicate hands against
Pharaoh's hard chest, stiffening her arms, and throwing herself back over the edge of the chariot. Use-
less efforts! vain struggles!

Her smiling captor drew her slowly and relentlessly
closer to his breast, as if he would glue her there;
she began to scream, he closed her lips with a kiss.

In three or four bounds the horses reached the
pylon, which they galloped through, glad to return to
the stable, and the car rolled into an immense court.
Grooms ran to the heads of the horses, whose bits
were white with foam.

Tahoser glanced around her with a frightened look:
high brick walls formed an enormous square enclosure,
within which rose upon the eastern side a palace,
and upon the western a temple, between two large
ponds, tanks for the sacred crocodiles. The first rays
of the sun, whose disk was just beginning to emerge

from behind the Arabian chain, cast a rosy glow over
the roofs of the buildings, the lower part of which
was still in a bluish shadow.

No hope of escape: the architecture, although there
was nothing sinister in its appearance, had about it
a character of irresistible strength, indomitable will,
and eternal inflexibility; a cosmic deluge alone could
have forced an opening in those thick walls, through
those masses of hard sandstone. To bring down
those pylons, made of quarters of mountains, the
planet would have to be shaken to its base; a conflagration could do no more than lick the indestruc-
tible blocks with its flames.

Poor Tahoser had none of these violent forces
at her disposal, and could not do otherwise than let
herself be carried like a child by Pharaoh, who had
leaped down from his chariot. Four high columns
with palm-leaf capitals formed the propylons of
the palace, through which the king entered, still
holding the daughter of Petamounoph in his arms.
When he had passed the portal he set his burden down
gently, and, seeing Tahoser stagger, said to her,—

" Be of good courage : you can rule Pharaoh, and
Pharaoh rules the world."

It was the first time he had addressed her.

If love were governed by reason, Tahoser would
certainly have preferred Pharaoh to Poëri. There
was something divine about the king's beauty : his
features, grand, pure, and regular, looked as if they
had been chiselled, and it was impossible to discover

in them any imperfection. The habit of command had given to his eyes that penetrating look that distinguishes divinities and kings. His lips, a word from which could change the face of the world and the fate of nations, were of a crimson bright as blood just shed upon the blade of a sword, and had, when he smiled, the grace of the terrible that naught can resist. His tall figure, well proportioned and majestic, presented the nobility of outline that we admire in the statues of the temples; and when he appeared, grave and radiant, covered with gold, enamels, and precious stones, in the midst of the blue smoke of the amschirs, he did not seem to belong to that frail race which, generation after generation, falls like the leaves, and is laid away, saturated with bitumen, in the impenetrable darkness of the tombs. In comparison with this demi-god, what was the miserable Poëri? And yet Tahoser loved him.

Wise men long ago ceased trying to understand the heart of woman. They have conquered astronomy, astrology, and mathematics; they know the birth-theme of the universe, and can tell the position of the planets as far back as the creation of the world; they are sure that at that time the moon was in the sign of Cancer, the sun in the Lion, Mercury in the Virgin, Venus in the Balance, Mars in the Scorpion, Jupiter in Sagittarius, and Saturn in Capricornus; they have traced upon papyrus and granite the course of the celestial ocean, from east to west; they have counted the stars, sown upon the

blue robe of the goddess Neith, and have made the
sun travel through the upper and lower hemispheres,
with the twelve diurnal and the twelve nocturnal
barks, under the guidance of the hieracocephalous
pilot, and Neb-wa, the Lady of the bark; they
know that in the latter half of the month Tôbi,
Orion acts upon the left ear, and Sirius upon the
heart; but they cannot tell why a woman should
prefer one man to another, a miserable Israelite to
an illustrious Pharaoh.

After passing through several apartments with
Tahoser, whom he led by the hand, the king sat
down upon a chair in the form of a throne, in a
magnificently decorated room.

The blue ceiling sparkled with golden stars, and
against the pillars supporting the cornice stood statues of kings, wearing the pshent, their legs engaged
in the stone, and their arms crossed upon their
breasts, while their eyes, outlined with black, stared
into the room with a startling intensity.

Between every two pillars a lamp was burning
upon a pedestal, and the panels on the walls represented a sort of ethnographical procession.

The nations of the four quarters of the globe were
represented there with their distinctive physiognomies and peculiar costumes.

At the head of the series, led by Horus, the shepherd of the people, marched the man *par excellence,*
the Egyptian, the Rot-ñ-no, with gentle face, slightly-
aquiline nose, braided hair, and dark-red skin inten-

sified by the white cloth about the loins. Following these came the negro, or Nahasi, with his black skin, thick lips, prominent cheek-bones, and woolly hair ; then the Asiatic, or Namou, flesh-color, verging upon yellow, with a decidedly hooked nose, full black beard trimmed to a point, and wearing a gaudy kilt with a tasselled fringe; and last of all, the European, or Tamhou, the most barbarous of all, distinguished from the others by his white complexion, blue eyes, red hair and beard, tattooed arms and legs, and the untanned ox-hide thrown over his shoulder.

Scenes of war and victory, with hieroglyphic inscriptions explaining their import, filled the other panels.

In the midst of the chamber, on a table supported by figures of captives with the arms bound together, so admirably sculptured that they seemed to live and suffer, an enormous bouquet of flowers spread itself, the suave perfume filling the air.

Thus, in this magnificent apartment surrounded by the effigies of his ancestors, everything told the story of Pharaoh's greatness ; the nations of the world followed upon Egypt's heels, acknowledging her supremacy, and he was ruler of Egypt : still, the daughter of Petamounoph, far from being dazzled by all of this splendor, was thinking of Poëri's villa, and above all of the miserable hut of clay and straw, in the Hebrew quarter, where she had left Rachel, happy Rachel, now the sole betrothed of the young Hebrew.

Pharaoh held Tahoser by the tips of the fingers as

she stood before him, and fixed upon her his falcon-like eyes with their motionless lids: the young girl had no other dress than the drapery that Rachel had substituted for the robe that had been soaked in the Nile, but her beauty lost nothing thereby; she was half naked, holding with one hand the stuff that kept slipping down, and the upper portion of her charming figure was uncovered in all its fair golden coloring.

When she was adorned, one could not but regret that any of her beauty should be marred by neck-laces, bracelets, belts of gold, and precious stones; but seeing her thus, stripped of all ornament, admiration was sated, or rather exalted.

It was true that many beautiful women had entered Pharaoh's gynecæum; but none were to be compared with Tahoser, and the king's eyes shone with such a light that her own fell before their radiance.

In her heart Tahoser was proud of having excited Pharaoh's love: for where is the woman, perfect though she may be, who has no vanity?

And yet she would rather have followed the young Hebrew into the desert. The king terrified her; she was dazzled by the grandeur of his appearance, and her legs would scarcely support her. Pharaoh, who saw her agitation, made her sit down at his feet on a red embroidered cushion ornamented with tassels.

"O Tahoser," said he, kissing her dark locks, " I love you. When I beheld you from my triumphal palanquin, borne above the heads of the people by the oëris, a strange sensation shot through my soul.

I, whose every desire was anticipated, longed for
something at last: I understood that there was something in the world besides myself. Until then I had
lived alone in my omnipotence, in the heart of my
gigantic palaces, surrounded by smiling forms calling
themselves women, who awakened as little sympathy
on my part as the painted figures of the frescoes. I
could hear from a distance the faint groaning and
sighing of the nations upon whose heads I had wiped
my sandals, or that I had borne off by the hair, as
they represent me doing in the symbolic bas-reliefs
of the pylons, but in my chest, cold and hard as that
of a god of basalt, I could not hear the beating of
my heart. It seemed to me that there was no being
upon earth that was like me and that could have any
attraction for me. In vain I brought back with me,
from my expeditions into strange countries, fair young
girls, and women celebrated in their own land for
their beauty: after having admired them for a time
I cast them aside as I would a flower. Not one of
them awakened within me a desire to see her again.
Present, I scarcely bestowed a glance upon them;
absent, they were quickly forgotten. Twéa, Taia,
Amensé, and Hont-Reché, whom I retained from a
disinclination to seek for others who to-morrow would
have suited me no better, were never anything else
in my arms than perfumed, graceful beings, vain
phantoms, and creatures of another race, with whom
it was as impossible for my nature to assimilate as
for the leopard and gazelle to agree, or the denizens

of air and water; and I began to think that the gods having set me beyond the reach of mortals, I could not share their joys and sorrows. A profound ennui, like that which must attain the mummies, swathed in their bandages, and resting in their coffins, down in the tombs, till their souls have accomplished the circle of migrations, took possession of me upon my throne, where many a time I laid my hands upon my knees, like a granite colossus, meditating upon the impossible, the infinite, and the eternal. Often I thought of raising the veil of Isis, at the risk of being struck dead at the feet of the goddess. 'Perhaps,' I mused, 'this mysterious face is the face that I have dreamed of, the one that will inspire my love. If earth refuses me happiness, I will scale heaven.' But I beheld you; I experienced a novel and peculiar sensation; I became conscious that outside of me there existed a necessary, fatal, and imperative being that I could not do without, and that had the power to make me unhappy. I was a king,—a god, almost; O Tahoser! you have made of me a man!"

Never perhaps had Pharaoh said so much at once. Usually a word, a gesture, a lowering of the eyelid, noted by a thousand anxious and watchful eyes, sufficed to make known his will. His thoughts were carried into execution as speedily as the thunder-bolt follows the lightning. It seemed to Tahoser that he had laid aside his granite-like majesty; he spoke, he expressed himself like a mortal.

Tahoser was prey to a strange agitation. Although

18

she was sensible of the honor of having inspired the love of the favorite of Phré, the beloved of Amon-Ra, the ruler of nations, the terrible, solemn, and superb being towards whom she scarcely dared raise her eyes, she found nothing sympathetic in him, and the idea of belonging to him filled her with an unconquerable dread. To this Pharaoh who had taken possession of her body by force she could not yield her soul, that was still with Poëri and Rachel, and, as the king seemed waiting for a reply, she said,—

"How has it come to pass, O king, that among all of the daughters of Egypt your choice should have fallen upon me, that so many surpass in beauty, talents, and all manner of gifts? Why, amid the clusters of expanded pink, blue, and white lotus-flowers, with their insinuating fragrance, have you selected a poor blade of grass, that has nothing to distinguish it?"

"I cannot tell; but I know that you are all the world to me, and I will make the daughters of kings your servants."

"And if I do not love you?" said Tahoser, timidly.

"What does it signify, so that I love you?" responded Pharaoh. "Have not the most beautiful women in the world cast themselves upon my threshold, weeping and sighing, lacerating their faces, beating their breasts, and tearing their hair, imploring with their last breath one look of love which was not granted? The passion of others never made this heart of brass palpitate within this marmorean breast. Resist me, hate me, I shall only find you more charming: it is the first time that my will has met with an obstacle, and I shall conquer it."

"And if I love some one else?" continued Tahoser, emboldened.

At this suggestion Pharaoh knit his brows; he bit his nether lip fiercely, leaving the white marks of his teeth in it, and pressed the young girl's fingers, that he still held, until he hurt her; then, growing calm again, he said, in deep and measured tones,—

"When you have lived in this palace, in the midst of so much splendor, surrounded by the atmosphere of my love, you will forget all, like those who eat nepenthes. Your past life will appear to you like a dream, all your former feelings will pass away like incense upon the charcoal of the amschirs: the woman who is loved by a king has no recollection of other men. Go and come, accustom yourself to Pharaonic magnificence, take all of my treasures that lie in your way, make the gold flow in streams, collect the jewels in heaps, issue your commands, make and destroy, humiliate and exalt, be my wife, my mistress, and my queen. I give you Egypt, with its priests, its armies, its laborers, its innumerable inhabitants, its palaces, its temples, its towns; riddle it as you would a piece of gauze; I will find you other kingdoms, grander, richer, and more beautiful. If the world does not satisfy you, I will conquer the planets and dethrone the gods. You are the only being that I love. Tahoser, the daughter of Petamounoph, exists no longer."

CHAPTER XIV.

WHEN Rachel awoke she was surprised not to find Tahoser beside her, and she gazed around the room, supposing that the Egyptian had already arisen.

Tamar, squatting down in one corner with her arms crossed upon her knees and her head resting upon this bony support, was asleep, or rather pretending to be; for through her tangled gray locks that fell to the ground you could see her eyes, yellow as those of an owl, twinkling with malicious pleasure and evil satisfaction.

"Tamar," cried Rachel, "what has become of Tahoser?"

The old woman, as if suddenly aroused by her mistress's voice, stretched her spider-like limbs languidly, rose to her feet, rubbed her brown eyelids several times with the back of her yellow hand, wrinkled as a mummy's, and asked, with a well-feigned air of astonishment,—

" Is she not here?"

" No," answered Rachel; "and if I did not see the dent that she has made in the bed beside me, and the robe that we took off from her hanging upon yonder peg, I would think that the strange events of last night were but the illusions of a dream."

Although she had made up her mind what ground

to take concerning Tahoser's disappearance, Tamar
put aside the curtain hanging in one corner of the
room, as if the Egyptian might be concealed there,
opened the cabin door, and, standing on the sill,
looked carefully about in every direction, then, turning towards her mistress again, shook her head.

"It is strange," said Rachel, pensively.

"Mistress," said the old servant, approaching the
beautiful Israelite in an insinuating and coaxing
manner, "do you know that I did not like this
stranger?"

"You do not like any one, Tamar," replied Rachel, smiling.

"Except yourself, mistress," said the old creature,
carrying the young woman's hand to her lips.

"Oh, I know you are devoted to me."

"I have never had any children, and sometimes I
feel as if I were your mother."

"Good Tamar," said Rachel, affectionately.

"Was I wrong," continued Tamar, "when I
thought it strange in her to come? Her disappearance proves that I was not. She called herself
Tahoser, daughter of Petamounoph : it was only a
demon that had assumed this form to tempt a child
of Israel and lead him astray. Did you see how
disturbed she was when Poëri denounced the idols
of stone, wood, and metal, and how difficult it was
for her to pronounce the words, 'I will try to believe
in your God'? One might have thought that the
phrase was a red-hot coal in her mouth."

"The tears that she shed upon my bosom were real tears, the tears of a woman," said Rachel.

"Crocodiles can weep when they wish to, and hyenas laugh to attract their prey," continued the old woman: "the evil spirits that prowl about among the rocks and the ruins are up to every trick, and can take any shape."

"Then, according to your way of looking at it, poor Tahoser was only one of the imps of darkness."

"Certainly," replied Tamar. "Is it a very likely thing that the daughter of the great priest Petamounoph would fancy Poëri, and prefer him to Pharaoh, whom they pretend is in love with her?"

Rachel, who did not consider any one superior to Poëri, did not think it such an improbable thing.

"If she loved him as much as she professed to, why did she run away when, with your consent, he agreed to take her as his second wife? It was the condition of renouncing false gods and worshipping Jehovah that put to flight this devil in disguise."

"At all events," said Rachel, "this demon had a very sweet voice and a very mild look."

In reality, Rachel was not very disconsolate over Tahoser's disappearance. She now owned the entire heart of which she had been willing to yield a portion, and the merit of the sacrifice still remained.

Under the pretext of going for provisions, Tamar went out, directing her steps towards the palace of the king, for her cupidity had not lost sight of his

promise; she was armed with a big gray linen bag
to be filled with gold.

When she presented herself at the palace gate the
soldiers did not beat her any more: she was now of
some importance, and the oëris on guard admitted
her at once. Timopht led her before Pharaoh.

When he beheld the repulsive old hag crawl-
ing towards his throne like an insect that has been
trodden upon, the king remembered his promise, and
commanded that one of his granite rooms should be
thrown open to the Jewess, so that she might take
away all the gold she could carry.

Timopht, whom Pharaoh trusted and who knew
the secret of the lock, opened the stone door. The
immense heap of gold shone in the sunlight, but
there was no more brilliance in the gleam of the metal
than was in the old woman's glance; her eyeballs grew
yellower, and glittered strangely. After a few moments of stupefied contemplation, she pulled up her
patched sleeves, uncovering her dried-up arms, a mass
of wrinkles inside the elbow, with the muscles standing out like cords; then she opened and shut her
hooked fingers, that were like the claws of a griffin,
and darted upon the pile of golden coins with a vulgar
and savage eagerness.

She plunged her arms up to the shoulders among
the ingots, took them up in handfuls, shook them,
let them roll about, and threw them up into the air;
her lips quivered, her nostrils dilated, and nervous
chills coursed up and down her spine. Intoxicated,

insane, all of a tremble, and giggling convulsively, she stuffed her bag, saying, "More! more! more!" until it was filled to overflowing. Timopht, amused at the sight, let her go on, never imagining that the gaunt old witch could lift such an enormous weight; but Tamar fastened her bag at the top with a string, and, to the amazement of the Egyptian, slung it upon her back. Avarice lent unusual strength to the wasted body : every muscle, every nerve, every fibre of the neck, arms, and shoulders was stretched until it was ready to snap under the weight of a mass of metal that would have bent the strongest porter of the Nahasi race ; with her head bowed down like that of an ox when the ploughshare encounters a stone, and her legs tottering beneath her, Tamar left the palace, almost walking upon all-fours, for sometimes she rested her hands upon the ground so as not to fall under her burden : at last she was outside, and the bag of gold belonged to her.

Breathless, exhausted, streaming with perspiration, her back broken, and her fingers cut, she sat down upon her treasure; and never had she tried a more luxurious cushion.

Before long she discovered two Israelites passing with a hand-barrow, on their way back from carrying some burden to its destination : she called them to her, and, after promising a good reward, persuaded them to take charge of the bag and follow her.

The two Israelites, preceded by Tamar, threaded their way through the streets of Thebes till they

reached the plains, dotted with mud hovels, in one
of which they deposited the bag. Tamar gave them,
grudgingly, the promised reward.

In the mean time, Tahoser had been installed in a
magnificent apartment, a royal apartment, as splendid
as that of Pharaoh. Elegant columns with the lotus
capitals supported a starry ceiling framed in a cornice
of blue palmettos traced upon a golden lacquer; pale
lilac panels, bearing green stems, ending in a bud,
decorated the walls. A fine matting covered the
marble floor; divans incrusted with metal scales alternating with enamels and upholstered with a material
that had a black ground strewn with red circles,
fauteuils with lions' feet, and a cushion rolling over
the top, stools resting upon swans' throats interlaced,
piles of purple-leather cushions stuffed with thistle-
down, seats that would accommodate two, and tables
of precious woods, supported by figures of Asiatic
captives, composed the furniture.

On richly-sculptured pedestals stood immense
golden vases and mixing-bowls of inestimable value,
the workmanship surpassing the material. One of
them, tapering away at the base, rested upon two
horses' heads, arching under their fringed trappings;
stems of the lotus, falling gracefully over rosettes,
formed the handles; ibexes held the cover upon their
ears and horns, and upon the sides hunted gazelles
were running through the papyrus reeds.

Another, quite as remarkable, had, in the shape
of a cover, an enormous head of Typhon, wreathed

with palms, and grinning between two serpents; the sides were ornamented with leaves and denticulated bands.

One of the mixing-bowls, uplifted by two individuals in mitres, wearing robes with wide borders, and supporting the base with one hand and the handle with the other, excited amazement on account of its enormous size and the elegance and perfection of the ornamentation.

Another, of a simpler and purer form perhaps, had a graceful swell, and jackals, placing their paws upon ·the edge as if about to drink from it, formed the handles with their slender, lithe bodies.

Metal mirrors surrounded by disfigured faces, as if to afford the beauty gazing therein the pleasure of contrast,—chests of cedar or sycamore wood, painted and decorated,—caskets of enamelled ware, jars of alabaster, onyx, and glass, boxes of aromatics,—all proved the lavishness of Pharaoh towards Tahoser.

With the precious things that this room contained, one could have ransomed a kingdom.

Seated upon an ivory chair, Tahoser was looking at the stuffs and jewels spread out before her by young girls who were displaying the treasures contained in the chests.

Tahoser had just left the bath, and the perfumed ointments with which they had rubbed her lent elasticity to the fine, soft texture of her skin. Her flesh had the transparency of agate, and the light seemed to shine through it; she was divinely beautiful, and when she fixed her eyes, brightened with antimony, upon the polished metal of the mirror, she could not help smiling at the image reflected there.

A wide gauze robe enveloped her charming figure without concealing it, and her only ornament was a necklace of lapis-lazuli hearts, surmounted by the cross and depending from a string of gold beads.

Pharaoh appeared upon the threshold of the room : a golden asp bound his thick locks, and a calasiris, with the pleats brought forward so as to form a point, covered his body from the belt to the knees. A single gorget encircled his neck, with its powerful muscles.

When she saw the king there, Tahoser was about to rise from her seat and prostrate herself before him ; but Pharaoh came forward, raised her up, and made her sit down again.

" Do not humiliate yourself thus, Tahoser," said he, in a gentle voice : " I wish you to be my equal : I am tired of being alone in the world. Although I can do all things, and have you in my power, I will wait until you can love me as if I were no greater than other men. Put aside all fear ; be a woman, with her will, her sympathies, her caprices : I have never seen anything of the kind ; and if your heart should plead for me at last, give me, when I enter your room, the lotus-flower in your hair."

In spite of all he could do to prevent it, Tahoser

dropped upon her knees before Pharaoh, and a tear fell upon his naked foot.

"Why does my heart belong to Poëri?" she mused within herself as she took her place again upon the chair of ivory.

Timopht, raising one hand to his head and lowering the other to the ground, now entered the apartment.

"O king," said he, "a mysterious person demands an audience with you. His immense beard descends to his waist; there are shiny protuberances like horns upon his bald forehead. A strange power precedes him; all the guards make way for him, and all the doors stand open. What he orders must be done; and I was obliged to come to you and disturb your happiness, even though I should suffer death for my audacity."

"What is his name?" demanded the king.

"Moses," replied Timopht.

CHAPTER XV.

THE king passed into another room to receive Moses, and seated himself upon a throne with arms shaped like lions. He fastened a large pectoral about his neck, grasped his sceptre, and assumed a pose of superb indifference.

Moses appeared: another Hebrew, named Aaron, accompanied him. August as Pharaoh was upon his golden throne, surrounded by his oëris and bearers of flabella, in that room with its high ceiling supported by enormous columns, and its painted walls representing his own great deeds and those of his ancestors, Moses was no less imposing: the majesty of age in this instance equalled the royal majesty. Although he was eighty years of age, he seemed full of manly vigor, and there was nothing about him indicating decay or senility. The lines in his forehead and cheeks were like incisions in granite, making him appear venerable without establishing his age; his brown and wrinkled neck was attached to his broad shoulders by lean but still powerful muscles, and a net-work of thick veins covered his hands, that did not tremble like those of an old man.

A stronger spirit than the human spirit animated his body, and his face shone, even in the shadow, with

K   19

a singular light, that seemed like the reflection of an invisible sun.

Without prostrating himself, as was customary when approaching the king, Moses advanced towards Pharaoh's throne, saying,—

"Thus saith the Lord God of Israel: Let my people go, that they may hold a feast unto me in the wilderness."

Pharaoh replied, "Who is the Lord, that I should obey his voice to let Israel go? I know not the Lord, neither will I let Israel go."

Not intimidated by the king's answer, the stately old man repeated with great distinctness, for the hesitation that troubled him formerly had disappeared,—

"The God of the Hebrews hath met with us; let us go, we pray you, three days' journey into the desert, and sacrifice unto the Lord our God, lest he fall upon us with pestilence, or with the sword."

Aaron bowed his head, confirming Moses' words.

"Why do you take the people from their work?" demanded Pharaoh. "Get you unto your burdens. Happily for you, I am in a clement mood to-day, or I should have had you beaten with rods, your noses and ears cut off, and your living bodies thrown to the crocodiles. Know, even as I now declare it to you, that there is no other god but Amon-Ra, the supreme and primordial being, at the same time male and female, his own father, and his own mother, of whom he is also the husband; from him descend all the other gods that unite heaven and earth, and that are only different forms of the two constituent principles: the wise men know it, and the priests, who have long studied the mysteries in the colleges, and within the temples consecrated to the divers representations. Do not bring forward another god of your own invention to incite the Hebrews to revolt and prevent the completion of the work they are engaged upon. Your pretext of sacrifice is transparent: you want to escape. Depart from before my face, and continue to make brick for my royal and sacerdotal buildings, for my pyramids, my palaces, and my walls. Go: I have spoken."

Moses, seeing that he could not move Pharaoh's heart, and that if he insisted he should only excite his wrath, retired in silence, followed by the dismayed Aaron.

"I have obeyed the commands of the Lord," said Moses to his companion, when they had passed out through the pylon; "but Pharaoh remained as insensible as if I had been addressing one of those men of granite seated on thrones at the palace gates, or those idols with the head of a dog, an ape, or a hawk, before whom the priests burn incense in the temples. What shall we say to the people when they ask us how we succeeded?"

Pharaoh, fearing that the Israelites might take it into their heads to shake off the yoke if they should listen to Moses, made them work harder still, and refused them straw to mix with their bricks. So the

children of Israel went about Egypt pulling up the
stubble and cursing the taskmasters, for they were
very unhappy, and they said that the schemes of
Moses had only increased their misery.

One day Moses and Aaron appeared again at the
palace, and once more challenged Pharaoh to suffer
the Israelites to go into the desert and sacrifice to
the Lord.

"How can you prove," demanded Pharaoh, "that
you are indeed sent by the Lord to tell me these
things, and that you are not, as I suspect, only vile
impostors?"

Aaron threw down his rod before Pharaoh, and
the wood began to twist and writhe, to clothe itself
in scales, to move the head and tail, to erect itself,
and to hiss horribly.

The rod had become a serpent. Its coils rattled
upon the slabs, and, dilating its throat, thrusting out
its forked tongue, and rolling its red eyes about, it
seemed to be looking for a victim to strike.

The oëris and attendants about the throne were
paralyzed and speechless with fright at the sight of
such a miracle. The bravest had partly drawn their
swords.

But Pharaoh was not in the least disturbed; a
disdainful smile flitted over his lips, and he said,—

"So this is all that you have to show me. The
miracle is insignificant, and the trick commonplace.
Summon my wise men, magicians, and hieroglyphists."

They appeared: they were persons of formidable and mysterious aspect, with shaven heads, and papyrus sandals on their feet, wearing long linen garments, and carrying canes engraved with hieroglyphics: they were yellow and dried up like mummies, from late hours, study, and an austere manner of living; the fatigue of successive initiations had set its seal upon their countenances, no part of which seemed alive but the eyes.

They took their places in a line before Pharaoh's throne, without paying any attention to the serpent that was still writhing, stretching out its neck, and hissing.

"Can you," demanded the king, "turn your sticks into reptiles, as Aaron has just done in our presence?"

"O king, is it for this child's play," said the most venerable one of the band, "that we have been called from our cells, where, under starry ceilings, by the light of lamps, we meditate, leaning over undecipherable papyri, kneeling before obelisks with their hieroglyphics of deep and mysterious meaning, unravelling the secrets of nature, calculating the power of numbers, laying our trembling hands upon the hem of the veil of great Isis? Let us return; for life is short, and the learned has barely time to pass over to his successor the problem he has solved; suffer us to go back to our work: the first juggler, the *psylle**

---

* *Psylle*, serpent-charmer.

who sounds his flute in the squares, will perform what you ask."

"Ennana, do what I have demanded," said Pharaoh to the leader of the hieroglyphists and magicians.

Old Ennana turned towards the college of sages, who stood there motionless, their minds already buried again in the abyss of meditation.

"Throw your sticks upon the ground, and pronounce the incantation."

The canes fell from their hands upon the stone floor with a clatter, and the wise men resumed their perpendicular pose, like that of the statues leaning against the pillars of the temples; they did not even deign to glance down at their feet to see whether the miracle had been accomplished, so sure were they of the formula.

It was a strange and horrible spectacle : the canes curled up like green twigs in the fire; their extremities flattened out into heads, or tapered away in tails,—some remaining smooth, and others growing scaly, according to the kind of serpent. Here they rattled, there they rose up erect; on this side they hissed, and on that wound through themselves, making hideous knots.

There were vipers bearing the mark of an iron lance on their bruised heads, cerastes with their threatening horns, greenish and slimy hydras, asps with movable fangs, glass snakes, yellow trigonocephali, crotalidæ, with short nose and black skin, sounding their rattles, amphisbænidæ moving backward and forward, boas opening their huge jaws wide enough to swallow the bull Apis, serpents with their eyes encircled by disks like those of the owl : the floor of the room swarmed with them.

Tahoser, who was sitting beside Pharaoh upon his throne, drew her beautiful, naked feet up under her, pale with terror.

" Well," said Pharaoh to Moses, " you see that the skill of my hieroglyphists equals or surpasses your own : their sticks have produced serpents like that of Aaron. Therefore, if you wish me to believe in you, perform some other miracle."

Moses extended his hand, and Aaron's serpent sprang upon the twenty-four reptiles. The struggle did not last long ; it soon swallowed the fearful animals, apparent or real creations of the Egyptian magicians ; then it resumed the form of a stick.

This result seemed to astonish Ennana. He bowed his head, pondered, and finally said, like one who has weighed the subject,—

" I will discover the word and symbol. I have not interpreted aright the fourth hieroglyphic of the fifth perpendicular line where the conjuration of serpents is to be found."

" O king, is our presence still required ?" asked the chief hieroglyphist, haughtily. " I would fain resume my reading of Hermes Trismegistus, which contains secrets of a very different character from these tricks of legerdemain."

Pharaoh made a sign to the old man that he was permitted to retire, and the silent cortège disappeared again in the depths of the palace.

The king re-entered the gynecæum with Tahoser.

The daughter of the priest, still frightened and trembling on account of what she had witnessed, knelt before him and besought him,—

" O Pharaoh, do you not fear to irritate by your resistance this unknown God to whom the Israelites want to celebrate a feast a three days' journey from here in the desert? Suffer Moses and his people to perform their rites, or it may be that the Lord, as he is called, will punish Egypt, and we shall die."

" What! has this serpent-jugglery alarmed you ?" exclaimed Pharaoh ; " did you not see my magicians also turn their sticks into reptiles ?"

" Yes, but Aaron's devoured them all, and it is a bad omen."

" What does it signify ? Am I not the favorite of Phré, and the beloved of Amon-Ra ? Have I not the figures of the conquered upon my sandals ? When it pleases me, I will sweep out of sight with a breath all this Hebrew race, and we shall see whether their God can protect them !"

" Have a care, Pharaoh," returned Tahoser, who remembered what Poëri had said concerning the power of Jehovah : " do not let pride harden your heart. Moses and Aaron fill me with dread: to have braved your displeasure they must be supported by a very terrible God !"

"If their God were so powerful," said Pharaoh, in answer to Tahoser's fears, "would he leave them in bondage, humble and uncomplaining as beasts of burden under the severest tasks? Let us forget these idle miracles and dismiss all anxiety. Think only of my love for you, and believe that Pharaoh has more power than the Lord, this visionary divinity of the Hebrews."

"Yes, I know that you are the subduer of nations, the controller of thrones, and that men are no more in your path than grains of sand blown about by the southern wind," replied Tahoser.

"And yet I cannot make you love me," said Pharaoh, smiling.

"The ibex is afraid of the lion, the dove dreads the hawk, the eye cannot gaze at the sun, and I am still bewildered and terrified in your presence; human weakness cannot accustom itself at once to the majesty of a king. A god always frightens a mortal."

"You make me regret, Tahoser, that I was not the first in your affections, whether as an oëris, a monarch, a priest, an agriculturist, or even something still more humble. But, if I do not know how to make a man of a king, I can make a woman a queen, and I will deck your fair brow with the golden viper. The queen will no longer fear the king."

"Even though you should place me beside you on your throne, in my thoughts I would still be kneel-

P

ing at your feet. But you are so good, in spite of your supernatural beauty, your unlimited power, and the effulgence surrounding you, that perhaps my heart will take courage and dare to beat in response to yours."

It was thus that Pharaoh and Tahoser discoursed: the daughter of the priest could not forget Poëri, and sought to gain time by flattering the passion of the king with a little hope. To escape from the palace and go to rejoin the young Hebrew was an impossibility. Poëri, on the other hand, accepted her love rather than shared it. Rachel, notwithstanding her generosity, was a dangerous rival. And then Pharaoh's tenderness touched Tahoser: she would have been glad if she could have loved him, and perhaps she was not so far from it as she fancied.

CHAPTER XVI.

SOME days later, Pharaoh was driving along the shore of the Nile, standing upright in his chariot and followed by his train of attendants,—he was on his way to see what degree the river had attained,— when Moses and Aaron appeared before him, in the midst of the road, like phantoms. The king reined in his horses, that had already shaken the foam from their bits upon the chest of the stately and motionless old man.

Moses, with a slow and solemn voice, repeated his adjuration.

" Prove the power of your God by some miracle," replied the king, " and I will grant what you ask."

Turning towards Aaron, who followed him at a little distance, Moses said,—

" Take your rod, and stretch out your hand upon the waters of Egypt, upon their streams, upon their rivers, upon their ponds, and upon all their pools of water, that they may become blood ; and that there may be blood throughout all of the land of Egypt, both in vessels of wood and in vessels of stone."

Aaron lifted up his rod and smote the waters that were in the river.

Pharaoh's attendants awaited the result with anxiety. The king, who bore a heart of brass in a chest of granite, smiled scornfully, trusting to the skill of his hieroglyphists to confound these foreign magicians.

As soon as the rod of the Hebrew, that rod which had been a serpent, touched the river, the waters began to stir and seethe, their muddy appearance underwent a perceptible change : a reddish tinge manifested itself, then the whole mass became a deep crimson, and the Nile was turned into a river of blood, rolling high its scarlet waves and tossing a pink froth upon the shores. It looked as if it mirrored a tremendous conflagration, or a sky rent with lightning; but the atmosphere was calm.

Thebes was not on fire, and the unchangeable blue spread itself over this red stream dotted here and there with the white bellies of the dead fish. Long scaly crocodiles helped themselves up on the banks of the stream with their crooked legs, and ponderous hippopotamuses, like great blocks of red granite covered with a black leprous scum, fled through the rushes, or lifted their enormous muzzles above the surface, unable to breathe in the bloody water.

The canals, ponds, and pools were all of the same color, and the jars containing water were as red as the craters that receive the blood of victims.

Pharaoh was unmoved by this prodigy, and said to the two Hebrews,—

"This miracle may terrify a credulous and ignorant populace, but there is nothing in it that surprises me. Let Ennana and the college of hieroglyphists be summoned : they will perform the same trick."

The hieroglyphists, led by their chief, arrived : Ennana glanced at the river with its red waves, and knew what was required of him.

"Restore everything to its former state," said he to Moses' companion, "that I may work the same enchantment."

Aaron smote the stream once more, and it resumed its normal color.

Ennana made a sign of approval, like an impartial savant doing justice to the skill of a brother. He found the thing well done for one who had never had, like himself, a chance to study science in the mysterious chambers of the Labyrinth, where only a few of the initiated could enter, the tests were so severe.

"It is my turn now," said he. And he stretched out his cane, engraved with hieroglyphics, over the Nile, muttering some words in a language so old that it must have been unintelligible even in the time of Menes, the first king of Egypt; a language of the sphinx, with syllables of granite.

An immense red flood spread from shore to shore instantaneously, and the Nile began once more to roll onward with its bloody waves towards the sea.

The twenty-four hieroglyphists saluted the king as if about to retire.

"Remain," said Pharaoh.

They resumed again their impassible look.

'Have you no other proof to give of your mission but this? My wise men, as you see, imitate your enchantments without any trouble."

Not disconcerted by the irony of the king, Moses said to him,—

" In seven days, if you do not suffer the children of Israel to go into the desert so that they may sacrifice unto the Lord according to their ceremonies, I will return and perform another miracle in your presence."

At the end of seven days Moses returned. He repeated to his servant Aaron the words of the Almighty,—

" Stretch forth your hand with the rod over the streams, over the rivers, and over the ponds, and cause frogs to come up upon the land of Egypt."

As soon as Aaron had stretched forth his hand, millions of frogs came up from river, canal, stream, and marsh; they covered the fields and the roads, hopped up the steps of the temples and palaces, invaded the sanctuaries and the most retired apartments; and new legions were ever following after the first: the houses were full of them, the kneading-troughs, the ovens, the chests; one could not plant his foot anywhere without crushing one; as if on springs, they jumped between the legs, on the right, on the left, forward and back. Away in the distance you could see them plashing about, leaping, clambering over each other, for already there was scarcely room for them, and their ranks closed together, and were heaped and piled one upon another : out in the country their innumerable green backs looked like fresh and verdant meadows, in which their yellow eyes were the flowers.

The animals, horses, asses, and goats, irritated and frightened, fled across the fields, only to encounter on all sides this unclean germination.

Pharaoh, who contemplated from the threshold of his palace the rising flood of frogs, with an air of disgust and annoyance, crushed as many as he could with the end of his sceptre and pushed away others with the curved toe of his sandal. Vain efforts! new-comers, springing from one could not tell where, replaced the dead, more lively, more noisy, more unclean, more troublesome, and more daring ; thrusting out their spinal columns, fixing their great round eyes upon him, spreading out their webbed feet, and wrinkling their white throats. The repulsive creatures seemed endowed with intelligence, and the layers were thicker about the king than elsewhere. The living tide rose higher and higher; on the knees of the colossi, on the cornices of the pylons, on the backs of the sphinxes and criosphinxes, on the entablatures of the temples, on the shoulders of the gods, on the pyramidal points of the obelisks, the hideous little beasts, with their backs hunched up and their toes spread out, had taken up their position. The ibises, which had rejoiced at first over this unexpected windfall, prodding them with their long beaks and swallowing them by the hundreds, now began to be alarmed at the prodigious invasion, and flew up towards the zenith, clapping their bills.

Aaron and Moses had triumphed; Ennana, being summoned, seemed to be lost in thought. With his fingers upon his bald brow and his eyes half closed, he looked as if he were searching in his mind for some forgotten magic formula.

Pharaoh, annoyed, turned towards him.

"Well, Ennana! by dint of dreaming have you lost your mind? And is this miracle beyond your power?"

"By no means, O king; but when one measures the infinite, computes eternity, and unriddles the incomprehensible, he may happen not to have at his tongue's end the strange sentence that has power over reptiles, bringing them into existence or destroying them. Behold now! All of this vermin shall disappear."

The old hieroglyphist waved his wand, muttering a few syllables.

Immediately the fields, the squares, the quays, the streets of the city, the palace-courts, and all the rooms in every house were rid of their croaking occupants and restored to their original condition.

The king smiled, proud of the skill of his wise men.

"It is not enough to have dispelled Aaron's enchantment," said Ennana: "I am now going to repeat it."

Ennana waved his wand in an opposite direction,

and pronounced a different formula in an undertone.

The frogs instantly reappeared in greater number than ever, jumping about and croaking; and in the twinkling of an eye the land was covered with them. But Aaron stretched out his rod, and the Egyptian magician could not remove the invasion brought about by his own enchantments. It was in vain that he repeated the mysterious words, the incantation had lost its power.

The college of hieroglyphists retired, abashed and thoughtful, pursued by the vile plague. Pharaoh wore an angry frown; but he was still obdurate, and would not hearken to the prayer of Moses. His pride would hold out to the end against this unknown God of Israel.

However, not being able to rid himself of the ugly reptiles, Pharaoh promised Moses that if he would intercede for him before his God the Hebrews should be permitted to go and sacrifice in the desert.

The frogs died or returned to the water; but Pharaoh's heart grew hard again, and, in spite of Tahoser's gentle remonstrances, he did not keep his promise.

And now all manner of plagues and scourges were let loose upon Egypt; a mad struggle took place between the hieroglyphists and the two Hebrews, whose prodigies they imitated. Moses converted the dust of Egypt into insects, Ennana did likewise. Moses took two handfuls of ashes and threw them up toward heaven, as he stood before Pharaoh; and immediately a red pestilence broke out, and the skin of the Egyptian people was covered with an eruption that did not touch the Hebrews.

"Imitate this miracle," said Pharaoh, beside himself with rage, his face as red as though the flames of a furnace were shining upon it, to the chief hieroglyphist.

"Where would be the use?" responded the old man in a discouraged tone of voice: "the finger of the Unknown is in all of this. Our vain formulas are of no avail against this mysterious force. Submit to it, and suffer us to return to our sanctuaries, that we may study this new God, this Almighty One more powerful than Amon-Ra, than Osiris, and than Typhon. The science of Egypt is surpassed; the enigma guarded by the Sphinx is meaningless, and the great Pyramid covers but an empty void, with its enormous mystery."

As Pharaoh still refused to let the Hebrews go, all the cattle of the Egyptians died; but the Israelites did not lose one.

A south wind rose and blew all night, and when the day dawned an immense reddish-brown cloud veiled the entire sky: through this tan-colored mist the sun glowed like a buckler in the forge, and seemed to be stripped of its rays. This cloud was different from any other cloud; it was alive, there was a rustling sound through it, and a fluttering of wings, and at last it descended upon the earth, not in great drops

of rain, but in layers of pink, yellow, and green
locusts, more numerous than the grains of sand in
the Libyan desert; they followed each other in whirlwinds, like straws before the tempest; the air was
dark and dense with them; they filled the ditches,
the ravines, the watercourses; they extinguished with
their numbers the fires kindled for their destruction;
where they encountered an obstacle they collected in
heaps about it until they surmounted it.

If you opened your mouth, one was sure to enter;
they lodged in the folds of your garment, in the hair,
in the nostrils; their thick ranks drove back the
chariots, knocked down solitary wayfarers, and soon
hid them from sight. The formidable army, jumping
and flying, went up and down over Egypt, from the
cataracts to the Delta, covering an immense extent
of land, mowing down the grass, reducing the trees
to skeletons, eating up the plants to their roots, and
leaving nothing behind them but the ground, bare
and empty as a threshing-floor.

At the prayer of Pharaoh, Moses caused the
plague to disappear; an east wind, of great violence,
carried all the locusts into the Red Sea; but this
stubborn heart, harder than brass, porphyry, and
basalt, would not relent.

Hail, a scourge unknown to Egypt, fell from the
sky, amid blinding flashes of lightning and deafening peals of thunder, its enormous stones cutting
and breaking everything before them and levelling
the wheat like a scythe; then a black, opaque, and

frightful darkness, in which the lamps went out as they do in the depths of the tombs, where there is no air, settled down with its black clouds over the land of Egypt, so fair, so luminous, so sunny beneath its azure sky, whose night is clearer than the day in other climates. The terrified people, believing themselves already enclosed within the impenetrable darkness of the sepulchre, groped their way along, or sat down beside the propylons, moaning and rending their garments.

One night, a night of terror and gloom, a spirit passed over Egypt, entering each house whose doorway was not stained with blood, and all the first-born male children died, the son of Pharaoh as well as the son of the most miserable parischite. Yet the king, in spite of all these terrible signs, would not yield.

He remained within his palace, silent and unapproachable, gazing at the body of his son extended upon the funeral bier with jackals' feet, unconscious of the tears with which Tahoser bathed his hands.

Moses loomed up on the threshold of the room without waiting to be announced, for the servants had fled in every direction, and repeated his demand with imperturbable solemnity.

"Go," said Pharaoh, at last, "and sacrifice to your God as you like."

Tahoser threw her arms around the king's neck, and said,—

"I love you now: you are a man at last, and not an image of granite."

CHAPTER XVII.

PHARAOH did not answer Tahoser; he was still gazing gloomily at the corpse of his eldest son; his indomitable pride rebelled even while it relented. In his heart he did not believe in the Lord, and was sure that the plagues with which Egypt had been smitten were due to the magic power of Moses and Aaron, which excelled that of his hieroglyphists. The idea of submitting infuriated this fierce and unyielding heart; but even if he had wished to keep the Israelites, his terrified people would not have permitted it; the Egyptians, through fear of being killed, would have united in chasing away these strangers who had been the cause of all their troubles. They avoided them with a superstitious dread, and when the stately Hebrew passed, followed by Aaron, the bravest among them took to their heels, fearing some new marvel, and saying to each other,—

"What if the rod of his companion were to turn into a serpent again and twine itself around us?"

Had Tahoser forgotten Poëri when she threw herself upon Pharoah's neck? By no means; but she felt that projects of vengeance and extermination were springing up in this obstinate soul. She was afraid of massacres which would include the young Hebrew and the gentle Rachel, a general slaughter

which would turn the waters of the Nile this time
into real blood, and she tried to soften the wrath of
the king with caresses and affectionate words.

The funeral cortège came and took the body of
the young prince to bear it away to the Memnonia
quarter, where it must undergo the process of embalming that lasted seventy days. Pharaoh witnessed its departure with a sad look, and said, as if
under the influence of a melancholy foreboding,—

"My son is gone, O Tahoser; and if I die now
you will be queen of Egypt."

"Why speak of death?" said the priest's daughter: "year after year will pass without leaving any
trace of their flight upon your strong physique, and
generations will fall around you as the leaves do
about a tree that still stands upright."

"I, the invincible, have I not been overcome?"
replied Pharaoh. "What does it avail though the
bas-reliefs represent me, armed with scourge and
sceptre, driving my war-chariot over the slain, or
bearing off conquered nations by the hair, if I am
obliged to yield to the sorceries of two foreign magicians, if the gods to whom I have raised so many
enormous temples, constructing them to endure to
eternity, do not defend me against the unknown
God of an obscure race? The prestige of my power
is gone forever. My hieroglyphists, reduced to
silence, have abandoned me; my people murmur;
I am no longer anything but a mere image: I have
willed, and have not been able to carry my will into

effect. You were right when you said it a moment
ago, Tahoser : I have descended to the level of mankind. But, since you love me, I will try to forget
these things, and will marry you as soon as the
funeral ceremonies are over."

Fearing that Pharaoh would repent of his promise, the Hebrews made ready for their departure, and
soon their cohorts were in motion, led by a pillar of
cloud by day and a pillar of fire by night. They
proceeded on their way into the wilderness lying
between the Nile and the Red Sea, avoiding the
nations that might oppose their progress.

The tribes one after another defiled past the statue
of copper, the work of the magicians, which had the
power to stop slaves in their flight. But this time
the charm, infallible for centuries, did not act : the
Lord had destroyed its power.

The immense multitude advanced slowly, covering
a great area with their flocks and herds, their beasts
of burden weighed down with the riches they had
borrowed from the Egyptians, and dragging along
the enormous baggage of a people moving in a body
from one country to another : the human eye could
not reach either the front or the rear of the column,
disappearing from sight in both horizons behind a
cloud of dust. If any one had seated himself at
the roadside, to wait until the entire army filed by,
he would have seen the sun rise and set more than
once : they passed, and still they passed.

The sacrifice to the Lord was merely a pretext :

Israel was leaving the land of Egypt forever, and Joseph's mummy, in its painted and gilded coffin, accompanied them, borne upon the shoulders of porters, who relieved each other.

But Pharaoh was full of wrath, and he determined to pursue the Hebrews who were making their escape. He had six hundred war-chariots prepared, summoned his captains, clasped about his waist his girdle of crocodile's skin, filled the quivers of his chariot with arrows and javelins, put the brass guard upon his wrist to prevent it from being grazed by the bow-string, and started after them, taking with him a vast army of soldiers.

Terrible in his anger, he urged his horses to their utmost speed, and the six hundred chariots rolled after him with a brazen clatter, like terrestrial thunder. The foot-soldiers quickened their steps, but could not follow at such a furious pace.

Often Pharaoh was obliged to stop and wait for the rest of his army. During these halts he would strike the rim of his chariot with his fist, stamping with impatience, and grinding his teeth. He would lean forward, scanning the horizon in the hope of discovering through the clouds of sand raised by the wind some trace of the fugitive Hebrew tribes, thinking with fury how every hour increased the distance that separated them. If the oëris had not restrained him, he would have pushed onward without stopping, at the risk of finding himself alone against a whole nation.

It was no longer the green valley of Egypt that they were travelling through, but plains mammillated with shifting hills and striated with waves like the surface of the ocean: the earth's ribs were laid bare; anfractuous rocks, moulded into strange shapes, as if gigantic animals had rolled them under their feet when the ground was in a muddy state, at the time the world emerged from chaos, protruded here and there over the sandy waste, breaking at long intervals with their sharp peaks the even line of the horizon, melting into the sky in a belt of reddish haze. At enormous distances apart palm-trees shot up, spreading out their dusty fans near some spring, often entirely dry, whose basins the thirsty horses investigated with their bleeding nostrils. But Pharaoh, insensible to the fiery rain streaming down from a sky glowing at a white heat, soon gave the signal for a fresh start, and the cavalry and foot-soldiers were on the march again.

The carcasses of oxen or beasts of burden, lying upon their sides, with the vultures flying in circles above them, marked the route of the Hebrews, and kept the king's wrath alive.

An active army, used to marching, moves more swiftly than an emigrating nation dragging after them women, children, aged people, baggage, and tents: so the distance was diminishing rapidly between the Egyptian troops and the tribes of Israelites.

It was near Pihahiroth, on the Red Sea, that the Egyptians overtook the Hebrews.

The tribes were encamped along the shore, and when the people saw Pharaoh's golden chariot glancing in the sunlight, followed by his war-chariots and his army, they were so terrified they made a great outcry, and began to murmur against Moses who had brought them there to perish.

In fact, the situation was a desperate one. Before the Hebrews a line of battle; behind them the deep sea.

The women rolled upon the ground, tearing their garments, pulling out their hair, and beating their breasts. "Why did you not leave us in Egypt? Servitude is better than death, and you have brought us into the wilderness to die: were you afraid we should find no graves there?"

Thus the furious multitude reviled Moses, who continued impassible: the most courageous grasped their weapons and prepared to defend themselves; but the confusion was horrible, and the war-chariots rushing through this compact mass would make fearful havoc in it.

Moses, when he had cried unto the Lord, stretched out his rod over the sea; and then a miracle took place that no hieroglyphist could have imitated. An east wind arose and blew with such extraordinary violence that it furrowed the waters of the Red Sea as if it had been some gigantic ploughshare, casting up on the right and left salty mountains crowned with crests of foam. Divided by the force of this irresistible wind, that would have swept away the

Pyramids like grains of sand, the waters rose in liquid walls, leaving a wide road between them where one could pass over on dry ground: in their transparent depths, as though through thick glass, you could see the marine monsters writhing about, terrified by the daylight that had found its way down to the mysteries of the abyss.

The tribes hastened through this miraculous opening: a human torrent rushing between two steep banks of green water. The countless throng dotted the livid bottom of the gulf with black spots to the number of two millions, and left their footprints in the mud never grazed by anything but the belly of a leviathan. And the terrible wind still blew, passing over the heads of the Hebrews, whom it would have mowed down like grain, keeping back by its pressure the accumulation of roaring waves. It was the breath of the Almighty dividing the sea in twain!

Terrified by this miracle, the Egyptians were loath to follow the Hebrews; but Pharaoh with his haughty spirit that nothing could daunt, urging on his horses, which reared and fell back against the pole, and cutting them with a flourish of his whip with its double lash, his eyes bloodshot, and his lips covered with foam, roared like a lion when its prey is escaping, inducing them at last to enter upon this path so strangely opened.

The six hundred chariots followed: the last Israelites, among whom were Poëri, Rachel, and Tamar, gave themselves up for lost when they saw the enemy take the same route that they were passing over; but, when the Egyptians had gone some distance, Moses made a sign: the wheels of the chariots came off, and a horrible confusion ensued, horses and warriors fell upon top of each other and became entangled; then the miraculously-suspended mountains of water fell in, and the sea closed over, whirling about in a vortex of foam men, animals, and chariots, like straws tossed by an eddy in the current of a river.

Pharaoh stood alone in the floating shell of his chariot, and, intoxicated with pride and fury, shot the last arrows in his quiver at the Hebrews who had reached the other shore; the arrows exhausted, he took his javelin, and, already more than half engulfed, with one arm above the water, cast this impotent shaft at the unknown God, whom he still braved as he sank into the abyss.

A tremendous wave, rolling up two or three times over the shores of the sea, carried away the last fragments: of the glory of Pharaoh and of his army nothing remained!

And on the opposite shore, Miriam, the sister of Aaron, rejoicing, sang and played upon the timbrel, and all the women of Israel accompanied her with their instruments of onager-skin. Two million voices joined in the hymn of deliverance!

CHAPTER XVIII.

TAHOSER waited for Pharaoh in vain, and reigned over Egypt, but did not live long.

They laid her in the magnificent tomb prepared for the king, whose body could not be found, and her history, written upon papyrus, with the headings of the chapters in red characters, by Kakevou, scribe of the double chamber of light and guardian of the library, was secured at her side under the interlaced strips of muslin.

Was it Pharaoh or Poëri that she mourned? The scribe Kakevou does not say which, and Dr. Rumphius, who translated the hieroglyphics of the Egyptian scribe, would not take it upon himself to decide the question.

As for Lord Evandale, he has never cared to marry, although he is the last of his race. The young ladies cannot understand his coldness towards the fair sex, but would they in all likelihood ever imagine that Lord Evandale is in love retrospectively with Tahoser, daughter of the high-priest Petamounoph, who died three thousand five hundred years ago?

And yet there are English follies based upon less than the above.

THE END.

21*

MRS. WISTER'S POPULAR TRANSLATIONS

FROM THE GERMAN.

SEVERA.

From the German of E. Hartner.

12mo. Extra cloth. $1.50.

"This story is one of peculiar interest, and will be read with pleasure." —*Washington National Republican.* "It is one of the best of the long series of translations which Mrs. Wister has given us."—*Boston Transcript.* "The story is one of unusual merit." —*New England Journal of Education.*

THE EICHHOFS.

From the German of Moritz von Reichenbach.

12mo. Extra cloth. $1.50.

"A thoroughly pleasing romance, which will be read with well-sustained interest to the end."—*New York Evening Post.*

A NEW RACE.

From the German of Golo Raimund.

12mo. Extra cloth. $1.25.

"There is no translator so trusted by the public, or, indeed, who occupies any such position as that which Mrs. Wister's good work has secured for her. The book is a story rather out of the common course of German romances, and is drawn with great delicacy and finish."—*Publishers' Weekly, New York.* "A very interesting story."—*North American.*

CASTLE HOHENWALD.

From the German of Adolph Streckfuss.

12mo. Extra cloth. $1.50.

"She is one of the best German translators in America. 'Castle Hohenwald' belongs to the best class of German romances."—*Cincinnati Commercial.* "A brilliant and attractive story, full of incident and adventure, and sure to entertain the reader with its clever delineations of fashionable society."—*Boston Traveller.*

MARGARETHE;

Or, Life Problems.

From the German of E. Juncker.

12mo. Extra cloth. $1.50.

"'Margarethe' is eminently a romance of pure and elevating sentiments, and a work of high literary merit, as well as of absorbing and sympathetic interest. The story is one of great power."—*Boston Home Journal.* "A fascinating novel, extremely well written, handling characters, scenes, and dramatic incidents, as well as the weightiest 'life problems,' in a really masterly way. Few will feel like putting down the book when they have once began to read it."—*Baltimore Bulletin.* "This is the best novel that has appeared on our table for many a day. It is a book full of power, of beauty, and of thrilling interest."—*Cincinnati Commercial.*

MRS. WISTER'S POPULAR TRANSLATIONS
FROM THE GERMAN.

TOO RICH.
From the German of Adolph Streckfuss.
12mo. Extra cloth. $1.50.

"Novel readers will delight in the story as one of piquant flavor, and strong in development."—*Boston Evening Traveller.*

"Mrs. Wister's refined and pure taste never leads her amiss in making her selections, and the novel before us is quite as interesting as any of its predecessors of the same kind."—*Philadelphia Evening Telegraph.*

HULDA.
From the German of Fanny Lewald.
12mo. Extra cloth. $1.50.

"There is not a heavy page in the entire volume, nor is the interest allowed to flag from introduction to 'finis.'"—*Philadelphia New Age.*

"It is rare in these days of mediocre novels to find a work so thoroughly charming as this."—*Norristown Herald.*

"One of the most healthful, fresh, delightful, and artistically-constructed novels that has appeared this season."—*Philadelphia Evening Bulletin.*

A FAMILY FEUD.
From the German of Ludwig Hardner.
12mo. Extra cloth. $1.25.

"Few plots are more elaborately conceived or more graphically presented. From the first to the end the story grasps and holds the attention, and it is to be pronounced one of the best and most powerful novels recently issued. The tone of it is above any reproach, and its naturalness is to be altogether commended."—*Boston Evening Traveller.*

THE GREEN GATE.
From the German of Ernst Wichert.
12mo. Extra cloth. $1.50.

"It is a hearty, pleasant story, with plenty of incident, and ends charmingly."—*Boston Globe.*

"A charming book in the best style of German romance, redolent of that nameless home sentiment which gives a healthful tone to the story."—*New Orleans Times.*

"This is a story of continental Europe and modern times, quite rich in information and novel in plot."—*Chicago Journal.*

WHY DID HE NOT DIE?
Or, The Child from the Ebräergang.
From the German of Ad. von Volckhausen.
12mo. Extra cloth. $1.50.

"Few recently published novels have received more general perusal and approval than 'Only a Girl;' and 'Why Did He Not Die?' possesses in at least an equal degree all the elements of popularity. From the beginning to the end the interest never flags, and the characters and scenes are drawn with great warmth and power."—*New York Herald.*

"OUIDA'S" LATER WORKS.

IN MAREMMA.

A Story of Italian Life.

12mo. Extra cloth, $1.25; Paper cover, 60 cents.

" 'Ouida's' pen is a graphic one, and page after page of gorgeous word-painting flows from it in a smooth, melodious rhythm that often has the perfect measure of blank verse, and needs only to be broken into lines."—*Philadelphia Evening Bulletin.*

A VILLAGE COMMUNE.

A Story.

12mo. Extra cloth, $1.25; Paper cover, 60 cents.

"It is a book which claims and will repay a careful reading."—*Philadelphia North American.*
"It is deeply interesting with excellent character portrayal, the whole being written in the witty, sparkling style for which 'Ouida' is famous."—*Boston Post.*

"Consists of a passionate protest against the application to regenerated Italy of the *Code Napoléon.* The author draws a strong picture of the kind of oppression to which the peasants are now subjected."—*New York Times.*

MOTHS.

A Novel.

12mo. Extra cloth, $1.25; Paper cover, 60 cents.

"The present work is marked by all the bold originality in conception and quaint brilliancy of diction that characterizes all of 'Ouida's' books."—*Sunday Dispatch.*
"This is the latest contribution of the prolific and brilliant 'Ouida' to the literature of romantic fiction. The story moves more rapidly than that of 'Ariadne' or 'Signa,' and carries the reader's interest with it irresistibly to the end."—*Harrisburg Patriot.*
"Deserves to take rank by the side of the best of her previous novels. 'Ouida's' power of characterization, and her ability to sustain the interest of her stories from the beginning to the end, cause her books to be eagerly sought after by readers of fiction. She is a novelist of the intense school, with great descriptive and word-painting ability. Her plots are unique, yet not unnatural, and they are always skilfully developed, and the climax happily reached."—*Chicago Evening Journal.*

These Novels are universally acknowledged to be among the most powerful and fascinating works of fiction which the present century, so prolific in light reading, has produced.

"OUIDA'S" POPULAR NOVELS.

12mo.

Extra cloth, $1.25 per volume; Paper covers, 50 and 60 cents each.

GRANVILLE DE VIGNE;

Or, Held in Bondage. A Tale of the Day.

"This is one of the most powerful and spicy works of fiction which the present century, so prolific in light literature, has produced."

STRATHMORE;

Or, Wrought by His Own Hand.

"It is a romance of the intense school, but it is written with more power, fluency, and brilliancy than the works of Miss Braddon and Mrs. Wood, while its scenes and characters are taken from high life."—*Boston Transcript.*

CHANDOS.

"Those who have read 'Granville de Vigne' and 'Strathmore' will be sure to read *Chandos.* It is characterized by the same gorgeous coloring of style and somewhat exaggerated portraiture of scenes and characters, but it is a story of surprising power and interest." —*Pittsburgh Evening Chronicle.*

PUCK.

His Vicissitudes, Adventures, Observations, Conclusions, Friendships, and Philosophies.

"Its quaintness will provoke laughter, while the interest in the central character is kept up unabated."—*Albany Journal.*

IDALIA.

It is a story of love and hatred, of affection and jealousy, of intrigue and devotion. . . We think this novel will attain a wide popularity, especially among those whose refined taste enables them to appreciate and enjoy what is truly beautiful in literature." —*Albany Evening Journal.*

TRICOTRIN.

With Portrait of the Author from an Engraving on Steel.

"The book abounds in beautiful sentiment, expressed in a concentrated, compact style which cannot fail to be attractive, and will be read with pleasure in every household."—*San Francisco Times.*

FRIENDSHIP.

"Like all her books, it is intense and passionate; absorbing in plot and masterly in characterization."—*Boston Journal.*

IN A WINTER CITY.

"It is brilliant and characteristic."
—*Philadelphia Press.*
"This is one of the most fascinating of the recent works of this undeniably powerful novelist."—*New Haven Journal and Courier.*

UNDER TWO FLAGS.

A Story of the Household and the Desert.

"This is probably the most popular work of 'Ouida.' It is enough of itself to establish her fame as one of the most eloquent and graphic writers of fiction now living."—*Chicago Journal of Commerce.*

CHEAP EDITIONS OF POPULAR NOVELS.

ALTON-THORPE.

A Novel. By LUCY N. JANNEY. *Cheap Edition.* 12mo. Paper cover. 40 cents.

"The tone of the book is winning, and its sweetness, purity, and re- | finement cannot be too highly com- mended."—*North American.*

MARIE DERVILLE.

A Story of a French Boarding-School. From the French of Madame GUIZOT DE WITT, author of "Motherless," etc. Translated by MARY G. WELLS. *Cheap Edition.* 12mo. Paper cover. 40 cents.

"It is gracefully written, the moral is unexceptionably pure, the plot is very prettily evolved, and the characters | are drawn with delightful naturalness." —*Philadelphia Evening Bulletin.*

ALIDE.

An Episode of Goethe's Life. By EMMA LAZARUS, author of "Admetus, and Other Poems," etc. *Cheap Edition.* 12mo. Paper cover. 40 cents.

"This is a tender and touching love-story. The story is very charmingly | told, with rare grace and freshness of style."—*Boston Post.*

THROWN TOGETHER.

A Story. By FLORENCE MONTGOMERY, author of "Misunderstood," "Seaforth," etc. *Cheap Edition.* 12mo. Paper cover. 50 cents.

"A delightful story. There is a thread of gold in it upon which are | strung many lovely sentiments."— *Washington Daily Chronicle.*

JOHN THOMPSON,

AND OTHER STORIES. By LOUISA PARR, author of "Dorothy Fox," "Hero Carthew," "Adam and Eve," etc. *Cheap Edition.* Illustrated. 12mo. Paper cover. 40 cents.

"It is just the thing to pick up for a half hour's recreation, or to take on | a railroad journey."—*Philadelphia Evening Bulletin.*

WINGS.

A Novel. By JULIE K. WETHERILL. *Cheap Edition.* 12mo. Paper cover. 40 cents.

"It is a warm, passionate story of love and of sharp suffering. It is written with a steady, skilled hand, | is well constructed throughout, and is absorbingly interesting."—*New York Evening Post.*

LADY BELL.

A Story of the Last Century. By SARAH TYTLER, author of "Citoyenne Jacqueline," etc. *Cheap Edition.* With Illustrations. 12mo. Paper cover. 50 cents.

"A highly pleasing story of the last century, and ought to find many appreciative readers. It is a skilfully | told tale, with a capital plot and felicitously sketched characters."—*Philadelphia Chronicle-Herald.*

A Great Lady. A Romance. From the German of

Van Dewall. Illustrated. 8vo. Fine cloth. $1.25. Paper. 75 cents.

"*A Great Lady* is an excellent novel from the German of Van Dewall, by MS. The plot is absorbingly interesting, and the story is told with more of the brilliancy and spirit of a French than of a German novelist. Some of the incidents are related with a vivid dramatic power that calls for a high degree of praise. The principal character is drawn with remarkable vigor, and is original both in conception and development. The plot never loses its hold on the reader's attention. The style is terse, rapid, and picturesque." *—Boston Saturday Evening Gazette.*

The Atonement of Leam Dundas. A Novel. By

Mrs. E. LYNN LINTON, author of "Patricia Kemball," etc. 8vo. Illustrated. Cloth. $1.50. Paper. $1.00.

"Mrs. Lynn Linton's powerful novel, in which is unexpectedly developed an intensity of dramatic interest."— *Philadelphia Inquirer.* "This cleverly written story is one of the most charming contributions to the literature of fiction we have had for some time, and will repay perusal."—*New Orleans Bulletin.* "Mrs. Lynn Linton's story deserves a high place among sensation novels. . . . . This is an excellent work." *—London Athenæum.*

Philip Van Artevelde. A Dramatical Romance.

By Sir HENRY TAYLOR, author of "Edwin the Fair," etc. *New Edition.* 16mo. Cloth extra, red edges. $1.25.

"His dramas show, combined with true poetic feeling, the broad views and knowledge of human nature which have illustrated his long and useful official career."—*London Athenæum.* "A book in which we have found more to praise and less to blame than in any poetical work of imagination that has fallen under our notice for some time."—*Lord Macaulay, in the Edinburgh Review.*

Hubert Freeth's Prosperity. A Story. By Mrs.

NEWTON CROSSLAND, author of "Lydia," "Hildred, the Daughter," "The Diamond Wedding," etc. 12mo. Fine cloth, black and gilt ornamentation. $1.50.

"It is a carefully executed composition, and as such will be sure to commend itself to those epicures who like to enjoy their novel like their wine, leisurely, holding it up to the light from time to time, that they may see the rich color and mark the clear depth through the crystal. A high, healthy tone of moral teaching runs all through this book, and the story gains upon us as we continue it."—*London Times.*

Adam and Eve. A Novel. By the author of

"Dorothy Fox," "Hero Carthew," etc. 8vo. Extra cloth. $1.00. Paper cover. 60 cents.

"In delineation of character and in dramatic force it is remarkable."— *American Bookseller.* "The sympathetic power of its characterization, the bright naturalness of its dialogue, and the ingenuity of its plot make it one of the best novels of the season."—*Philadelphia North American.*

A Family Secret. An American Novel. By Fanny

ANDREWS ("Elzey Hay"). 8vo. Fine cloth. $1.50. Paper cover. $1.00.

"Her novel is as entertaining as any novel need be. . . . There are some character-drawing and life-picturing in the volume which mean a good deal more than mere amusement to discerning readers."—*New York Evening Post.*

"The character sketching and the narrative portions of the work are graphic and entertaining, and show considerable skill in construction on the part of the author. It is a book that will repay the reader's pains, and that is more than can be said of perhaps the average works of fiction."—*Boston Post.*

A New Godiva. A Novel. By Stanley Hope.

12mo. Extra cloth. $1.25. Paper cover. 50 cents.

"A capital story of English life, abounding in incident of a highly dramatic nature, and yet not overwrought. The plot is somewhat intricate, but it is clearly developed, and is decidedly interesting. The characters are well drawn, and the descriptive parts of the book are spirited and picturesque. There is enough excitement in it to do efficient service for two or three novels."—*Boston Saturday Evening Gazette.*

"It is written in a strong, skilled hand, confident of its strength, and conscious of its skill."—*New York Evening Post.*

"We heartily commend it to our readers."—*New Orleans Bulletin.*

Wild Hyacinth. A Novel. By Mrs. Randolph,

author of "Gentianella," etc. 12mo. Fine cloth. $1.50.

"One of the best novels of our day. No writer of fiction has produced a more delightful and interesting book."—*London Court Journal.*

"This is a clean, wholesome book. The plot, if slight, is very fairly good; the characters of the story are well drawn and skilfully developed; the moral is unexceptionable. . . . We have already said enough to show our hearty appreciation of a book which is excellent in tone and clever in execution."—*London Standard.*

Belles and Ringers. A Romance. By Hawley

SMART, author of "Courtship in 1720 and 1860," etc. 12mo. Extra cloth. $1.00. Paper cover. 50 cents.

"The characterization is spirited, and there is a genial freshness in the recital which makes it attractive reading throughout."—*Boston Saturday Evening Gazette.*

"It is fresh and breezy from beginning to end, without a dull page from cover to cover, and is written in such a captivating and cheery manner as to heartily commend it to all lovers of sound, healthy reading."—*Baltimore Gazette.*

Blanche Seymour. A Novel. By the author of

"Erma's Engagement." 8vo. Fine cloth. $1.25. Paper. 75 cents.

"It is simple and natural in plot, and is admirably told, particularly in its more pathetic portions. The sentiment is gracefully tender, and the characters are drawn with great spirit and discrimination."—*Boston Saturday Evening Gazette.*

"The author's great merit consists in the commendable naturalness of all her characters. She is, too, very amusing with her side remarks and the feminine cleverness which is to be seen on every page. . . . We hardly know a more entertaining little volume than this."—*New York Nation.*

The Heir of Malreward; or, Restored. A Novel.

By the author of "Son and Heir," etc. 8vo. Cloth. $1.50.
Paper. $1.00.

"This is an English story of ill-assorted marriage and the triumph of good over evil in what seemed to be irretrievably bad. It is a romance of no ordinary power."—*Chicago Evening Journal.*

Article 47. A Romance. From the French of

Adolph Belot. By JAMES FURBISH. 8vo. Cloth. $1.25.
Paper. 75 cents.

"An able translation of this brilliant and celebrated story, whose thrilling incidents and vivid scenes will amply repay perusal."—*Chicago Inter-Ocean.*
"A translation which created so profound a sensation when presented here in a dramatic form. The story will be read with interest. . . . It contains some remarkably powerful scenes, spiritedly told."—*Boston Saturday Evening Gazette.*

A Prodigious Fool. By John Calvin Wallis.

Small 12mo. Extra cloth. $1.25.

"The story of this life is told with much of graceful pathos in sentiment, and with considerable vigor of style."—*Boston Saturday Evening Gazette.*
"It is a capital story, with plenty of action and some quite telling in-cidents."—*Philadelphia Chronicle-Herald.*
"It is a very readable novel, that deserves encouragement."—*Pittsburgh Chronicle.*

Queenie's Whim. A Novel. By Rosa Nouchette

CAREY, author of "Wooed and Married," "Nellie's Memories," etc. 12mo. Fine cloth. $1.25. Paper. 75 cents.

"It is a bright, pleasant story of girl-life, told in easy, natural style, that leads one on from page to page with unflagging interest."—*Chicago Bookseller and Stationer.*
"It is certain to be immensely popular, and is highly commended to our readers."—*Baltimore Gazette.*
"Is an interesting picture of English domestic life, strong in its character-ization, and uncommonly animated and breezy in style. . . . The hero-ine is an admirable study. The story may be warmly praised for the purity of its tone, for the marked skill shown in its construction, and for the pleas-ing entertainment it affords."—*Boston Saturday Evening Gazette.*

One Woman's Two Lovers; or, Jacqueline Thayne's

Choice. A Story. By VIRGINIA F. TOWNSEND, author of
"The Hollands," "Six in All," etc. 12mo. Fine cloth. $1.50.

"This book must interest and hold the reader, and one will find much besides the plot and incident of the story to charm, as the evident study of nature and love for it shown by the authoress give many scenes of beauty to the book, and picturesque passages abound in it. It is a well-written and thought-out story, show-ing refinement and imagination, as well as a high ideal on the writer's part."—*Boston Evening Transcript.*